The Dating Secret

By B. N. Hale

27 Dates: The Series

The Dating Challenge

The Dating Secret

The Dating Game

The Christmas Date

The Valentine's Date

Table of Contents

Volume 8: The Fair Date

Chapter 1

Reed listened to his professor lecture about behaviors and drug effects. He enjoyed most aspects of his psychology degree, but the biology of the brain was less interesting. It didn't help matters that his thoughts were dominated by Kate, and the direction of their relationship.

He scribbled notes and then returned to the stupor shared by the other students in the class. Dr. Caldin spoke in a near monotone, a voice soft and dry, an invitation to fall asleep in the amphitheater classroom. Some had already succumbed. With the lights off, the glow of the projector could not compete with the pull of slumber. One student had been so audacious as to bring a pillow.

"Reed," a girl hissed from nearby.

He surreptitiously looked her way, but his caution was unnecessary. Dr. Caldin was staring rapturously at his slide, expounding the infinite complexities of the brain like they were the flavors of a savory meal.

"What do you need?" he asked, vaguely recalling the girl's name was Anna.

"Are you already taking someone out on Friday?"

He shook his head. "Why?" he whispered back.

"My roommate hasn't been out in months," she said. "I heard what you do and thought you'd like to take her out."

It was a request he'd heard a hundred times, sometimes by a girl wanting the invite for themselves. His response was now habitual, to inform them that he liked to meet and ask the girl out for himself, and a reminder of his rules. But as he opened his mouth the words lodged in his throat.

Since starting the dating challenge with Kate, his desire to date other girls had waned. Even though he avoided physical contact and intimacy, it still felt like a betrayal. But how could it feel like that if he was not dating Kate exclusively?

Anna was still waiting for the answer, but Dr. Caldin turned and surveyed the room, giving Reed a chance to further ponder his response. But all too soon the professor turned back to his slides and Anna glanced his way.

"I wish I could," he said, smiling in a self-deprecating manner, "but finals are next week and I'm grossly underprepared."

The girl nodded in understanding, but her eyes betrayed a flicker of disappointment. Guilt welled within him and he almost reached out to her. But although he sent the order to his arm, the limb did not respond.

Yet again, he considered if he was even capable of ending things with Kate. After their canceled date a week ago, when Kate had gone out with Jason, he'd sensed a shift in the tone of their conversations. They now texted and called almost daily, and he looked forward to such opportunities like a starving man did a piece of bacon.

Did he want to date her exclusively? Was he ready to abandon his other dates and devote his time to Kate? His heart warmed at the prospect, thumping in his chest and bringing a smile to his face. Jason was out of the picture, taking with him the lingering anchor he'd left in Kate's heart.

But even as Reed's heart warmed, a pit formed in his stomach. He'd made a promise to Aura and it remained unfulfilled. To date Kate as he wanted would mean abandoning his promise. The questions once again returned him to the impasse.

"Mr. Hansen?" a voice called his name.

He blinked and his vision focused on Dr. Caldin, who was staring at him, waiting expectantly. Several of the students were staring at Reed with amused expressions, revealing the professor had called on him more than once.

"Sorry, Dr. Caldin," he said, irritated that the kid on a pillow had not been called on. "My cerebral chemicals must have stopped."

The old man cracked a rare smile. "It happens to all of us," he said, and then called on another student.

The girl answered correctly, and the brief excitement diminished back to the previous stupor. Reed frowned, annoyed that he'd let his conflict impede his studies. He was usually very attentive in class, so the lapse came as a surprise to him and his friends, who cast him quizzical looks.

The clock ticked on the hour and Dr. Caldin dismissed the class. "Mr. Hansen?" he called amid the rush of papers and conversation. "May I speak to you for a moment?"

Reed stuffed his notebook into his laptop case and then shouldered the bag. Threading his way against the flow of escaping students, he reached the base of the classroom as Dr. Caldin turned off the projector.

"You seem distracted," Dr. Caldin said.

"I'm sorry," he said, "just thinking about my thesis."

"Still planning on graduating in December?"

Reed nodded. "Just summer classes and then I'll finish my thesis in the fall."

Dr. Caldin peered over his glasses. "Are you certain there is nothing else? Your clever response in class aside, I suspect your thoughts are not on your coursework."

Reed cracked a smile at the observation. "It might have to do with a girl."

"It always does," he replied. "And if it's intruding on *your* coursework, I suspect this particular girl is remarkable."

"She is," he said.

"Then don't let her go," Dr. Caldin said with a definitive nod. "Regret is the most abhorrent emotion."

"Is that going to be on the exam?" Reed asked.

Dr. Caldin regarded him with a knowing smile. "Not my exam, but grades in life matter more than in my class."

"Can I quote you?"

"I'll deny it," he replied, picking up his own laptop. "I'll see you next week, Mr. Hansen."

Reed watched him go with a faint smile. Most considered Dr. Caldin the quintessentially boring professor—which he was, in class—but Reed had gotten to know him during a semester as his teacher's assistant. The man harbored a dry sense of humor and wit that rarely manifested in front of a class. Privately, Reed suspected the man enjoyed putting his class to sleep and then calling on drowsy students, a game that provided amusement in the perpetually repetitive professor life.

Now alone, Reed ascended the classroom steps and stepped outside, blinking at the brilliance. The doors opened onto a large grassy area between buildings, the towering trees casting shade on the green expanse. Pockets of students sat beneath the trees, seeking to escape the afternoon heat as they prepared for upcoming finals. Groups were common, but a small crowd stood on the lawn outside the psychology building.

The group of forty turned to face him, swiveling as Reed appeared. All wore masks and carried water guns, the odd combination drawing attention from the scattered students. They drifted closer to the brewing conflict, pointing and smiling as they held up their phones to record. Reed spotted Dr. Caldin standing a short distance away, a slight smile on his face, as if he'd intentionally held him after class.

"Dr. Caldin?" he called. "I assume she got to you?"

"I admit nothing," he replied. "But you might want to leave your laptop behind."

Taking his advice, Reed removed his bag. By then the army of water gun toting students had arrayed themselves into a gauntlet, with another masked figure at the end. Most of the masks were from

Halloween, with a pair of wolfmen, a few zombies, and even a Darth Vader. The one waiting at the end wore a horned masquerade mask, but he recognized Kate's figure. She smiled and pulled a massive, four-foot envelope into view.

Fashioned from cardboard and painted to look like a letter, the envelope was clearly addressed to him. The implication was clear, that he had to run the gauntlet of water guns to get the message.

He grinned and removed his phone, tucking it into his laptop case to protect it. The act drew a round of laughter from those surveying the exchange and he noticed more with their phones out, clearly wanting to video the watery carnage.

"I suppose I have to run the gauntlet to get the invite?" he called.

The one in the masquerade mask smiled and nodded, and those with guns began pumping the handles, pressurizing their weapons. Reed began to laugh and readied himself for a sprint. Then he surged forward and forty masked attackers pulled the trigger, engulfing him in water.

Chapter 2

Water battered him and he gasped at the chill. He shielded himself with his arm, blocking his eyes as he ran. Shouts of delight rang out as he sprinted through the sprays, running blind. Eighty feet passed in a blur of water until Kate's voice brought him to a stop.

The water guns cut off and those viewing the spectacle began to applaud. Sopping wet and freezing in the warm May sun, Reed raised a hand and took a bow. Then he turned to Kate standing with the envelope, her smile rivaling the sun in the sky.

"Are you cold?" she asked innocently, her green eyes sparkling behind the masquerade mask.

"Freezing," he said, shivering. "Did you fill them with ice water?"

"Yes."

He laughed at the devious detail. Reed felt the attention of many eyes, but Kate's gaze held him bound. The laughter and applause faded into the background. Then she handed him the envelope and leaned up to kiss him on the cheek.

"Couldn't resist," she said mischievously.

She turned and strode away, taking most of her water gun toting army with her. Someone sprayed Reed in the back as he walked past, and Reed gasped, turning to find Jackson and Shelby with matching smirks. Both wore the masks from the last Halloween, the gladiator helmets sharp and angular.

"Did you have to join her on this invite?" Reed asked.

"Just obeying orders," Shelby said.

"I would have done it anyway," Jackson said smugly.

Shelby turned and sprayed him in the face, and then laughed as he stared in shock. Then his eyes gained a wicked gleam and he sprayed her back. In seconds the other erstwhile soldiers, eager for more, were quick to pick sides.

Reed dodged the hasty sprays and dragged the envelope back to his bag, out of reach from the furious melee. Water and shouts were hurled with equal measure, and the laughter spilled into the viewing crowd.

Reed wrung his clothes out and turned the envelope around to read the gigantic letters. In bold letters it gave a date and a time, followed by a cryptic invitation. Then Dr. Caldin appeared at his elbow to read it aloud.

"Guns, guns, everywhere and not a trigger to pull."

"It's a dating challenge," Reed explained.

"Oh, I already know about your little game," he said.

Reed raised an eyebrow. "When did you find out?"

"I already knew," he said. "I saw the article in the school paper and put two and two together. It was an invitation that matched your style, if a little more audacious than you prefer. It's about time a girl turned the tables on you."

"What do you make of this?" Reed asked, gesturing to the invite.

He smiled. "I suspect you are going to be using firearms. Do be safe. I'd like to hear how this particular story ends."

Reed gave a wry laugh and glanced at the water fight, which was rapidly ending as the weapons ran out of ammunition. He fleetingly wondered if his professor was standing next to him so Reed would not be drawn into the fight a second time. The old man's eyes certainly betrayed a sense of mischief.

"I'll see you next week, Dr. Caldin."

"Until next time, Mr. Hansen," he said, and strolled away.

Reed collected his bag and strode toward his car, leaving a trail of wet footprints on the sidewalk. The crowd began to disperse as the water fight came to a close, but several observers were still posting videos of the miniature war.

The video was probably already online, with anyone he'd ever dated getting a close-up view of him being soaked. He wondered what impact it would have on his future dating, and for the first time found himself grateful that he just had two semesters before graduation.

He passed students that eyed his sodden clothes with surprise, having not seen the incident. Then one smirked, suggesting he'd already seen the video. Reed grinned in turn as they walked by each other.

"Hope she's worth it," the guy said.

"The best ones always are," Reed said.

The student snorted, half in agreement and half in doubt. Then he went on his way, but Reed's own words lingered as he walked to his car. His feet squished, water leaking from his shoes with every step. A girl looked at him strangely at the sound, but he flashed a disarming smile and stepped to his car.

Then he spotted the towel tucked under the windshield wiper. He picked up the towel, pleased to find it warmed by the sun. He rubbed the soft material across his face and then pressed it against his shirt. As he dried himself the best he could without undressing, he marveled at the subtle gesture.

Kate could have left him to fend for himself, but she'd gone out of her way to leave a towel for him. He smiled as he placed the towel on his seat and sank into the driver's seat. For the moment he managed to push thoughts of Aura aside and toyed with the prospect of a future together with Kate.

Would she be his girlfriend? Would they still go on dates? Afraid of how much the idea appealed to him, he turned his thoughts to the coming week. He'd missed his chance to ask Kate on a date, so his next attempt had to be good. Although there were several ideas he'd contemplated, one stood out more than any other, and he smiled. It was three weeks away, plenty of time to schedule a tour.

He pulled into his driveway and withdrew his phone. After a quick Google search, he located the right website and browsed the tour times. Then he found the number and dialed. A moment later a pleasant-sounding woman picked up.

"Hidee Gold Mine."

He asked for Terry and when the man picked up the phone Reed smiled. He'd met Terry a few years ago at a tour of the mine and had gone back a couple of times. The old miner liked Reed and was more than happy to book another visit.

"What's the girl's name?" Terry asked.

"Kate," he said. "And she's a special one."

"Oh?"

Reed smiled at the amount of emotion the man managed to pack into a single syllable. "You'll see when you meet her," he replied. "I just want to plan something new."

"I'll figure it out," Terry replied.

Reed hung up shortly after and nodded to himself, excited at the prospect of taking Kate on such an unusual date. But it would have to be unique. He had no desire to repeat the same experience and he'd already been to a tour of the mine with other girls. Already brainstorming ideas, he exited the car just as Jackson and Shelby pulled into the driveway. All equally drenched, they squished their way to the house together.

"How did she get so many to help?" Reed asked.

"As you said," Shelby chuckled. "Everyone likes to be part of a romance."

"Is that why you help me when I ask a girl out?"

"Of course," Jackson said.

"I get to shower first," Shelby said.

"But I was the victim," Reed protested.

"I'm the girl," Shelby said with an apologetic shrug, ducking into the bathroom.

Jackson laughed. "She's got you there."

Reed grinned and strode to his room, the cooler air of the house already making him shiver. Deciding he couldn't wait for the shower, he stripped and dried before donning new clothes. When he stepped out he found Jackson also changed, albeit shirtless, sitting at the dinner table pouring himself a bowl of Fruity Pebbles.

"Can I ask you a question?" Jackson asked.

"You already did."

Jackson grunted in irritation, nearly spilling cereal from his mouth. Then he swallowed and said, "We both know how you feel about Kate. What's holding you back?"

Reed gestured dismissively, the habitual response coming with a disarming smile. But this time he found all the weight of indecision to be stifling. He stepped to the table and sank into a seat to stare at Jackson.

"You can't tell anyone—even Shelby."

Jackson raised an eyebrow, clearly surprised he'd gotten an answer. "Roommate's promise."

Reed looked away and listened to the shower run, wondering how he could possibly tell the whole story. But the words bubbled up like vomit, forcing themselves from his mouth. Before he could stop himself, he began to speak.

"Let me tell you about Aura . . ."

Chapter 3

Jackson sank back into his chair, his cereal forgotten in the bowl. Once Reed had begun speaking, the words had spilled from his lips in a frantic rush, until he'd finally fallen silent. The seconds passed but neither of them spoke until the shower turned off, causing Jackson to grunt.

"Wow."

"I know."

"I can't believe she . . ."

"I know."

Reed swallowed and looked away, all the pain of that night coming back in a flood of emotions. He realized his hands were clenched and forced his fingers to open. Jackson's expression was frozen in disbelief until he swept his hand to Reed.

"And you promised to . . ."

"A date for every second I listened to her die."

"That's . . ."

"Five thousand dates."

He balked. "Isn't that excessive?"

"She lost her life because of me," Reed said. "I swore I wouldn't let it happen to another girl."

Jackson regarded him for several seconds and then blew out his breath. "I need a drink."

"I'm sorry I didn't tell you."

"I understand why you didn't." Jackson shook his head and reached for his spoon, but the cereal had gone soggy. "What are you going to do?"

"I don't know," Reed said. "Please tell me you have some advice."

Jackson picked up the box of cereal and began to eat by hand, his expression twisted in thought as he munched. Again, the silence passed between them and then Jackson shook his head and shrugged.

"I've got nothing."

Reed frowned. "You're the first person I tell a massive secret to, and that's your answer?"

"I'm not very good with big issues," Jackson said. "When my grandfather died my mom got mad because I put my basketball in his casket."

"Really?" Reed asked.

Jackson grinned. "She demanded to know what I was thinking, and I said I thought he'd like to play in heaven."

Reed began to laugh. "I bet she hated that."

"She actually liked it," Jackson said with a smile. "She began to cry and said Grandpa would like the gift."

"So how exactly is your story supposed to help me?" Reed asked.

Jackson grabbed another handful of cereal. "You loved Aura, but I think she'd want you to be happy."

"So I should just let her go?"

"Why not?" Jackson asked, shoving the handful in his mouth.

Jackson's easy dismissal of years of regret brought a smile to Reed. He spoke with such simplicity, but Reed could not simply let go of his promise, even if he wished he could. He sighed and leaned back in his chair.

Shelby stepped out of the bathroom in a towel. "Shower's open," she called, and then spotted Reed and Jackson sitting at the table. "Is everything okay?"

"Great," Jackson said. "I was telling him about when my grandpa died."

"When you gave him your ball?" Shelby asked, shaking her hair out. "I think it was sweet."

"I should have given him my old one," Jackson said. "Grandpa was buried with my good ball."

Reed and Shelby shared a smile and she disappeared into Jackson's room to change. Jackson stood and shoved a final handful of cereal into his mouth. As he strode to the bathroom Reed called out to him.

"Please keep it to yourself."

"You think I want to share something like that?" Jackson jerked his head. "I'll leave the unloading of heavy knowledge to you. But you should tell Kate. I think she'd understand."

"It was hard enough to tell you," Reed protested. "And we've known each other for years."

"Doesn't matter," Jackson said, "I still think you should tell her."

He slipped into the bathroom, leaving Reed to his thoughts. Deciding to forego the shower, Reed reluctantly returned to his room. He collected his laptop on the way and threw himself into homework, hoping it would provide relief from his doubt. The homework didn't, but texting Kate did.

The next week passed in a blur of homework and preparation for finals week. In addition to tests, he had a pair of meetings with his thesis committee, the combination filling his time and providing a welcome distraction. He studied late and dreamed of homework, until finally completing the last of his exams the day of his date with Kate.

Excited, he texted her several times as he got ready. Then he waited outside for her. Jackson and Shelby were off celebrating with their basketball team, which had taken second in another competition.

19

Thoughts of Aura evaporated when Kate pulled into the driveway, and before she could get out Reed opened the door and sank into the seat. She grinned as he closed the door and gestured to him.

"Excited for tonight?"

"Let's just say I'd like to shoot something."

"That kind of week?"

He nodded. "Finals were tough. You?"

"I think I did fine," she replied, pulling onto the street. "And I got the internship for the summer."

Dressed in jeans and a plaid shirt, she looked every bit the country girl. She even wore a cowboy hat over her brown hair, making her rather cute. He said as much, and she smiled.

"This is not my usual style," she said. "But for today, it's only fitting."

"What will we be shooting?"

"Whatever you'd like," she replied. "Ember briefly worked at a shooting range because she liked a guy that worked there. She managed to talk him into providing us the evening."

"How romantic."

She laughed and pointed east. "We'll stop for dinner first. It's an odd place, but you can eat bison, alligator, even duck."

"I've never had any of those," Reed said.

"Me either," she said, "but I hear bison is good."

"Like a steak?" he asked, imagining carving into a gigantic steak.

"I think it's a burger," she said.

He grinned. "That sounds more my style."

As they drove into town they talked of food and favorites, and Reed enjoyed the easiness of the companionship. After the stressful week, just being with Kate was wonderful, and he found himself again trying not to hold her hand.

She too seemed unburdened. Although he thought it was due to the completion of her own finals, he began to guess it had more to do with Jason. They ate dinner and reminisced about the date with sushi, with both agreeing that a bison burger was better. When they climbed into the car again he rotated into his seat to look at her, finally deciding to voice his thoughts.

"You look good," he said, interrupting their conversation about favorite cheeses.

"I think you already said that," she said with a smile.

"Not your clothes," he said. "You. You look good."

Her eyebrows knit together. "Thank you?"

He grinned. "That sounded like a question."

"It was."

He shrugged, casting about for an explanation. "Since our first date there was a cloud hanging over you. Now it's gone."

"Until I met you, I regretted my choice to break up with Jason," she said. "I didn't understand everything that had happened between us. Between my dates with you and his return, I managed to put all my doubts to rest."

"And now?" he asked.

"I'm free," she said with a smile.

"And what do you plan to do with your newfound freedom?"

Her smile turned mischievous. "Shoot some guns."

"You said you used to shoot with your family?"

"I did," she said. "Military family, remember? I used to go with my dad and my brothers. I'm decent with a pistol, but I prefer rifles or shotguns. You?"

"Very little experience, I'm afraid. Although I used to go shotgun shooting when I was a scout."

"That's what your mother said."

Reed laughed lightly. "How many guys' parents have you talked to?"

"Only yours and Jason's," she said. "I think his mother didn't like me at first. Now that I think about it, his father didn't care for me either."

"Why?"

"I told you they were doctors, and they wanted him to marry one. I don't think an engineer was a prestigious enough occupation for their son."

"Sounds a little arrogant."

"Oh, I forgot to tell you," she said. "Jason said his parents are getting a divorce."

"That's too bad," he said. "How was he taking it?"

"Not well," she said. "He'd always considered his parents to have the model relationship. I think their falling apart left him shaken."

"It's always hard when your core principles are broken," he said, nodding. "Any younger siblings?"

"Three sisters," she said. "He's the oldest. The others are still in high school."

Reed winced. "So he now feels the weight of his family on his shoulders."

"I hadn't thought of that."

"Older siblings always feel a divorce the worst," he said.

Her eyes flicked to him and then returned to the road. "Is that you or your degree talking?"

"Both," he said. "My parents split up when I was a teenager, and all I wanted to do was protect my little sister."

"Now that you mention it," she said. "I think my older brothers did go out of their way to protect me. They used to get me candy when my parents were arguing and sneak me a tablet so I could watch TV."

"Clever."

"I may have fought with my brothers, but they were always on my side."

"You still sound sad."

She shook her head. "Not at my brothers. I'm just wondering—is that how every family is going to end up? With brothers protecting their sisters?"

"I hope not. But I guess it depends on the couple."

"Yes," she said, her eyes lingering on him. "I suppose it does."

Chapter 4

They pulled into the shooting range and parked next to the door. There was only one other car in the lot. Curious, Reed followed her to the door. Although a sign said the location was closed, she knocked and a moment later the door opened.

"Bart," she said.

"Kate," he said with a nod, ushering them inside. "I assume this is Reed?"

"It is," Reed said with a smile, offering his hand.

Bart took it and looked him up and down, the measuring look implying he'd heard about Reed, probably from Ember. Short and stocky, he had a wrestler's body but was already going bald, even though he appeared to be their age.

"Ever used a gun?" he asked, his accent marking him as native to Colorado.

"A few times," Reed said. "And I know enough to point the gun downrange."

Bart smirked. "You're halfway to safety right there."

He turned and led them into the darkened shop. Guns hung in cases against the wall, while boxes of ammunition, safety glasses, and other gear were stowed on shelves. A long counter ran down an entire wall and contained pistols and knives. On the back wall a pair of giant elk heads loomed over them, while targets marked every available inch of wall space. The range smelled of paper and gun oil.

"How's Ember?" Bart asked, leading them to the back, where he unlocked a door to lead them to the range behind.

"Less mad," Kate said, casting Reed an amused look. "Helping me tonight has erased much of her animosity."

"I swear that girl is more dangerous than a rifle," he said.

"Don't teach her to shoot," Reed said.

"That's why she's mad at me," Bart said with a rumbling laugh. "I started to teach her and she nearly shot me, so I took the gun away. She's mad because I refused to teach her again."

Reed grinned at the idea of the fiery Ember with a gun in her hands. It would be like giving a dragon a missile. Kate caught his eye and they stifled a laugh as they followed Bart through the maze of buildings.

The main structure fronted a series of small, outdoor ranges. As they passed the pistol range, a sign indicated the long-distance range was to the west. Trees surrounded the path, casting shade upon them and obscuring the view. A moment later the trail turned through a gap in the foliage and a hut came into view. A wide grassy area extended beyond the structure, the greenery spotted with orange and white fragments.

Bart sat them at a table and ran them through a brief safety talk. Then he motioned Kate forward. She picked up the shotgun and accepted the shell from him. With practiced fingers she loaded the weapon and took a step to the covered overhang looking out over the lawn. Bart picked up a remote and donned ear protection. Reed followed suit.

"Whenever you're ready," Bart said, his voice muffled.

She shouldered the weapon and then called, "Pull!"

Bart pushed the trigger and a clay pigeon shot from a window in the hut, soaring out over the field. Kate tracked it and fired, the report reverberating off the surrounding trees. But the clay pigeon remained unscathed until it shattered against a truck.

"Four more and then we'll trade," Bart said. "Let's see how many you can hit."

The answer was all four. Kate nodded in satisfaction as she lowered the shotgun, while the remains of her latest victim clattered to the ground. Then she turned to Reed and removed her ear muffs.

"Think you can do better?" she challenged.

"No," he said.

She laughed and handed him the gun. Donning his own safety glasses, he readied himself to lose. In short work he proved himself more capable than he remembered, finishing three of the five targets.

"Better than I expected," Kate said.

"Better than *I* expected," Reed said.

She laughed and they traded places. Bart ran the range until it became clear they could handle themselves. Then he departed to finish locking up. When he was gone, Reed took his turn on the gun.

"He's leaving us alone?"

"Ember let him know I came from a military family," she said. "Most of the clientele here is from the military, and they trust the shooters."

"It's Colorado," he said. "I'm surprised our state flag doesn't have a gun."

"Perhaps it should," she said with a smile.

"Pull!" he called. He fired and missed.

He'd accepted the fact that he was not going to best her, but he hoped he could at least keep from embarrassing himself. He couldn't. Her targets fell to her gun. His targets fell to the ground.

She stopped and rubbed her shoulder. "It's getting dark. Care to try pistols?"

"That depends."

"On what?"

"On how many things you want to prove you're better at?"

She laughed and placed the gun back in the case. "I told you I wasn't very good with pistols."

"Did I tell you how many times I've used a pistol?"

"How many?"

"If we shoot today? One."

She grinned and turned off the skeet launcher before heading back to the main structure. Bart set them up in the range and then disappeared back to the office. Shaped like a squat box, the interior shooting range contained motorized targets that could send a paper target to various distances.

Kate helped him load the pistol and then he took aim. At ten yards, he managed to hit the paper once, but nowhere near the center of the target. When he finished, she directed him to place the gun on the table and she took her turn.

The rounds echoed in the firing range, the sounds muffled through the ear protection. Reed watched the target at first but then his gaze was drawn to Kate, who stood with her body straight, her arms forward as she sighted along the gun. Her posture exuded strength, making her even more attractive.

She finished a clip and then put the gun down, smiling as she turned to him. "See? It's not so hard."

He swallowed the surge of desire and focused on the target, which now looked tattered across the paper. As he shook his head, they again traded places and she directed him on how to load the gun.

"Mind if I help?" she asked.

"I think I need it," he said ruefully.

She smiled and positioned his arms. "Put one foot behind the other and brace your arm like this. When you pull the trigger, don't pull too hard. It will twist the gun and cause it to jump to the side. Fire when ready."

She stood next to him, the side of her body pressed against his. Her arm was around his back, her touch feathery soft yet strong. He focused on the scent of burned gunpowder, hoping it would ground him.

"Ready?" she asked, her voice quiet, as if she'd suddenly recognized their proximity.

After three months of dating they had hardly touched, the absence now amplifying the desire to do so. Her hand on his elbow pulsed lightning into his arm and he shivered. He glanced her way and their eyes met, so close he could have kissed her if he just turned a few inches . . .

The door clattered open and Bart stepped in with several boxes of ammunition. Reed and Kate both jumped, and she stepped away with a flush. Reed was grateful he had the presence of mind to take his finger off the trigger as they parted.

"I only have a few more minutes," Bart said, placing the boxes under the table at the back of the range. "You about done?"

"I think so," Kate managed with a nod, glancing at Reed with a shy smile.

Bart pulled out his phone. "I'll give you five minutes," he said, obviously distracted.

"Thanks again, Bart," Kate said.

"Don't mention it," he replied, and then smiled, finally focusing on them. "At least to my bosses. Feel free to mention it to Ember."

"I will," she said.

He nodded and left, and in the ensuing quiet Reed looked to Kate. The moment had rattled them both, and Reed realized that after Jason's return and departure, the barriers between them had been partially removed. Reed tried to shrug it off with a smile but found he couldn't. He gestured to the gun in his hands.

"I'm not sure I got it."

She smiled, the expression tentative and surprised. Reed's request was a bending of his rules, an invitation for them to be physically close. A voice inside Reed wanted to protest as she took up her former position, the touch more intimate than before because he'd allowed it, because he wanted it.

"Ready?" she asked softly.

"I hope so," he said.

Chapter 5

Reed's clip lasted seconds, but the sensation of her against his side seared into his memory. Neither of them spoke of the encounter but Reed sensed a shift in their relationship. Up until this point they had kept a discreet distance, but now they'd come to a line of demarcation. He knew it wouldn't be the first time they did. The question would be, when would they cross?

"Did you enjoy shooting?" she asked as they left the range.

"A great deal," he said, choosing his words carefully.

She smiled, clearly pleased. "Every Christmas I go shooting with my brothers."

"Most people open presents."

"We do that too," she said. "Going shooting with them was a way for them to include me. Their lives are very different from mine, but an interest in guns was always something we shared."

"Who is the best shot?"

"Depends on who you ask," she replied with a laugh. "Each brother will say they are."

"And what would you say?"

"My oldest brother is Baker, but we call him Bake. He's a Marine and by far the strongest. And I'd say he's the best shot. My second oldest is Tyler. He's the smallest of my family and close to my size. But what he lacks in stature he makes up for in intelligence. He decided to join the Air Force and went to the Academy here in Colorado."

Reed recalled her mentioning her family on their first date, but it seemed like ages ago. "And the last brother?"

"Orin. He's the only one not in the military," she said. "But he always did march to the beat of a different drum. He's a mechanic at a shop outside of Memphis."

"I bet they were protective of you," he said.

Her eyes lit with amusement. "One guy tried to grab my chest on a date to a football game. Bake found out and had a conversation with him in the parking lot. I thought the guy was going to go home with broken bones. He never touched me again. Come to think of it, he never spoke to me again."

"I hope he still had his teeth."

"Bake is very intimidating," she said. "But only on the outside. He's a teddy bear on the inside."

"A teddy bear that can kill you."

She cast him an amused look. "Are you worried?"

Reed considered his answer. If their relationship did turn exclusive, he was probably going to meet her family at some point. Until now he'd kept a professional distance from the families of his dates, and he wondered how he would be received.

"Not worried," he said. "But I'd be stupid not to be cautious. It's clear they care about you a great deal."

"I couldn't ask for better siblings," she said.

She pulled onto the freeway and headed back into town. The sun had already set but the horizon glowed red and orange. Most of the cars already had their lights on and she activated hers. Several times he noticed her stealing looks his way, her eyebrows pulled together as if in confusion. He guessed it was because of the moment at the range.

Kate drove them to the eastern edge of town, and as they got off the exit he spotted the twinkling lights of a fair. Complete with a small Ferris wheel and other rides unloaded from trucks, the traveling fair was packed with people.

"The fair?" he asked, raising an eyebrow.

"I thought it would be fun," she said. "This particular one has a lot of shooting games, so consider what we just did as practice. Now you need to win me a bear."

He grinned as they pulled into a grassy parking lot and found an open space. Reed stepped into the warm air and was immediately surrounded by the scent of popcorn and the sound of laughter. Noticing his smile, Kate gestured to rides.

"Memories?"

"When I was a kid there was a fair that came every year," he said. "They had a giant zipline that felt like flying."

"I love the fair," she said as they fell into step together. "All the sights and smells."

Reed put his hands into his pockets so he wouldn't be tempted to hold her hand. If she noticed the gesture, she gave no sign. She paid their entrance and they walked down the center of the fair, enjoying the sights.

Tents and carnival style games interspersed the rides, which were surprisingly large for a traveling fair. The enormous Ferris wheel and tilt-a-whirl seemed to be favorites, while a spinning ride and a hall of mirrors were also popular.

"Hungry?" she asked.

"Yes," he said.

They stopped at a hot dog vender, which proved to have dozens of toppings including bacon, peas, corn, potato chips, and even chocolate. Several kids were eating chocolate covered hot dogs while their parents looked on in disgust.

"Hot dog with bacon, please," he said.

"Same," she said with a smile.

With food in hand they strolled through the crowded fair. Reed savored the surprisingly tasty hot dog as he watched a pair of teenagers attempt to throw rings onto bottles, the rings inevitably bouncing away.

Small tents served caramel corn and cotton candy. Others provided burgers and fries. Parents struggled to contain their overactive children, while a handful of older couples seemed to be lost in memories.

"Ready for the first game?" she asked, pointing to the shooting gallery.

"I don't know if I can do any better," he said, but allowed himself to be lead to the booth.

Built to resemble a forest scene, the shooting gallery had country music blasting from speakers. Targets on deer, bear, and smaller critters dotted the trees and ground, and when hit they swung out of sight. The guns were surprisingly sophisticated, and showed point counters on a display.

"Step right up!" the man called as two players left with two hundred points each, earning themselves stuffed squirrels. "Do I have myself some shooters?"

Kate stepped to the first of the two guns and the man smiled, his eyes flicking to Reed. "Does the lady know how to use a gun?" he asked.

"Oh, the lady does," Reed said with a laugh.

The man led Kate to the right gun while Reed took his position at the left. "Two minutes on the clock," the man said, rattling off the rules with practiced ease. "Break a thousand and get a special prize." He pointed to the board behind him that depicted rewards for succeeding at varying levels.

She shouldered her rifle and took aim at a squirrel. "Smaller animals are worth more," she said.

"You assume I can hit them," he said, aiming at a deer.

"Let the hunt begin!" the man shouted, and the targets burst into view.

Kate swiveled, firing at a squirrel and then a badger before taking aim at a bird soaring in the background. Metal pinged in rapid succession, her gun never missing the mark. Reed missed as much as he hit, but found that, after the practice earlier, he did better. When a timer buzzed and all the targets flipped out of view, they both looked down.

"Woah," Kate said.

"You cracked 1,000," Reed said, dropping his gun back into the holster.

"I thought it would take us a few hours to come close," she said, throwing the man a confused look. "Marta's cousin said it was impossible."

"Not impossible," the man said, a smirk on his face as he pointed away from the range. "Are you ready for your reward?"

"It's not one of the stuffed animals?" Reed asked, gesturing to the hanging prizes.

"I'm afraid not," he said, leading them away from his booth and to the Ferris wheel across the way.

"This little lady got a thousand at the range," he said to the Ferris wheel operator.

The youth, who couldn't have been more than eighteen, smirked and gestured them to the front of the line. Bewildered, Kate tried to protest, but they were ushered onto the Ferris wheel and a moment later sent spinning upward.

"Hope you're not afraid of heights!" he called as they gradually climbed into the sky.

"I'm not," she said, and then noticed they were the only ones on the wheel.

She frowned and leaned over the edge of the bench as the wheel came to a halt—with them at the apex. The basket swung slightly at the abrupt stop and they both looked down. The operator looked up to them, his smile smug.

"Enjoy your time in the sky!" he called.

Reed stifled a smile as Kate called for answers, only to be met with silence. The operator leaned back and folded his arms, clearly content to watch them have time alone at the top of the wheel. Then she finally turned to Reed, her eyebrows knit in confusion.

"I'm not sure . . ." Then she noticed his expression and her eyes narrowed. *"You* did this?"

"I did," he said.

"You *hijacked* my date?" she asked, her voice going up an octave.

"I did," he said with a smile.

Chapter 6

"How did you do it?" she asked. "I had an entire plan."

"I know," he said, "but I convinced Ember to help me."

"Traitor," she said.

"I didn't get to take you out on my turn," he replied. "So I wanted to steal a few minutes from your date."

She began to laugh, the sound building as she leaned back, the motion causing the bench to rock. Grateful she wasn't angry, Reed reached under the bench and pulled out the bag he'd had Jackson stash for him.

"Cotton candy?" he asked.

"This doesn't mean you win," she said, her humor subsiding as she accepted the treat.

"I think it does," he said.

"How did you ever turn Ember?" Kate marveled.

He took a bite of his own cotton candy. "I told her I felt cheated, that Jason had stolen my date. I didn't want to break our tradition, so we concocted the plan to hijack your date. I'm glad you aren't angry."

"Some," she admitted. "But more surprised. I love the Ferris wheel but the line is always so long it takes forever."

"I know," he said. "Your mom said you'd always wanted to get stuck on the top of a Ferris wheel."

"How did you convince the fair to cooperate?"

He smiled. "That was the easy part. Marta's cousin was surprisingly helpful. I swear her extended family is like their own covert army."

She laughed again, the tone chagrined. "Do you get the feeling that our friends have no loyalty?"

"A little," he said. "But they want us to be happy."

"Is that what you are?" she asked, glancing his way.

He gestured to the view. With the lights of the fair below them, their vantage point allowed for an unbroken view of the valley below. The lights of Boulder were a dim glow beneath a starry night.

"How could I not be?" he asked.

"I never expected this challenge to occupy so much of my attention," she admitted. "I think about it in the morning, when I get ready for work, and in class. One of my professors asked why I was so distracted."

He nearly choking on cotton candy. "Dr. Caldin said that to me the day you soaked me. You were beautiful in the masquerade mask, by the way."

"You assume that was me?"

"I know your eyes," he said.

She raised an eyebrow and smiled coyly. "Oh? Just how well do you know my eyes?"

"Enough to know they're beautiful," he replied. "And I'll stop there before you think I'm stalking you."

"You called my mother and talked my roommate into hijacking my date," she said. "I think we're way past stalking."

"When you put it that way, you make it sound bad," he said.

"It's only stalking if I don't like it," she said. "And I assure you, I'm enjoying every minute with you."

Uncertain where to take the conversation, he smiled and looked at the view. The sun had set and the lights of the fair glowed beneath them. Then he noticed the crowd that had gathered below them. He expected them to be angry that the Ferris wheel was not moving, but most had smiles on their faces.

"It looks they are enjoying the spectacle," he said.

She leaned over the edge and smiled at the crowd. "They must think we're together."

"Kiss her!" someone shouted.

He grinned. "It looks like you're right."

Another person shouted as well, and it quickly swelled to a chant, the sheer volume drawing more people to the Ferris wheel. Employees leaned out of the tent and looked up, grinning as they joined the chant.

"Kiss her! Kiss her! Kiss her!"

She turned to him and tilted her chin upward in invitation, her eyes sparkling with mischief. "You set the stage," she said. "You have only yourself to blame."

"You're not going to help me out of this?" he asked.

"Nope," she said, her smile widening. "But I think if you don't make a move, they're going to riot."

He laughed, giving himself time to think. The crowd grew insistent, their chant rising with impatience. Kate cocked her head to the side as if waiting for the kiss, her smile one of invitation.

He grinned. "Don't move," he said, and then leaned in.

He put his arm around her and pulled her close. She blinked in surprise and shock but he twisted to the side, brushing his lips across her cheek. The contact was brief but sent tingles to his toes. More importantly, from the crowd it looked like a kiss, and they roared their approval.

He leaned back with a smug smile. "My apologies," he said.

"Cheater," she said.

It may have been his imagination, but it seemed she was breathless, and she swallowed several times as if attempting to regain her composure. He popped a bite of cotton candy in his mouth and tried to convince himself that he'd kissed her cheek exclusively for the moment. Then his eyes slid across the now dispersing crowd, and one face stood out.

Ember.

Standing with Marta, Brittney, Jackson, and Shelby, Ember stood in the center of the crowd, a smug smile on her face. She noticed him looking and their eyes met. Caught, she smirked and sauntered away, the others following. An ice-cream cone in hand, Jackson saluted as he left. A glance at Kate revealed she did not know the blondes were present. Reed may have sought to hijack Kate's date, but he was not alone.

Apparently deciding the kiss had ended the moment on a high note, the Ferris wheel operator pressed a button and they began to lower to the ground. Before their friends disappeared, Reed pointed to Ember.

"It appears that I wasn't the only one to hijack your date," he said.

It was clear the moment she spotted her roommate. "Ember," she said, spitting the word like a curse.

"It seems like she wanted to force a kiss," Reed said wryly.

Kate shook her head, and then grinned. "I'll have to thank her later."

"Me too," he said, drawing a surprised look.

"You're not mad she pushed your rules?"

"A little," he said, using her words. "But I can't deny how much I enjoyed it."

The Ferris wheel came to a halt and he stepped out, reaching back to help her from the bench. The crowd applauded as they walked back to the fair, and Reed endured the attention with a smile.

The rest of the night passed in a blur, but his thoughts remained on the almost kiss. It had been years since he'd kissed a girl, and the contact with Kate left an indelible mark. Obviously conscious that their relationship was pushing forward, Kate seemed content to accept the progress. But her looks made it seem she was examining him with new eyes.

Many times they were stopped so someone could shake their hands. One older gentlemen even smirked and tipped his hat. Enduring the scrutiny with grace, Kate smiled and gently dismissed assumptions even as she glanced at Reed, a twinkle in her eyes signifying she didn't entirely believe her own words. As the fair finally began to wind down, they returned to her car and she drove him home.

They talked, but he could not remember the words spoken. His lips continued to tingle with the yearning to pull her into his arms, and it took all his strength to hold the desire at bay. Only when she'd driven away and he stood on his porch did he allow himself to breathe.

"What do you think, Aura?" he murmured.

But there was no answer. Whether he meant it to happen or not, her grip on his soul had begun to loosen. Feeling lighter than he had in months, he turned and entered his house, already planning his next date.

Volume 9: The Rainy Date

Chapter 1

Kate trudged into the office building and pressed the button on the elevator. Yawning, she took it to the fourth floor and then wove through the maze of cubicles to her own desk. She sat down with a groan, causing Sara in the next cubicle to poke her head into view.

"Rough night?"

With glasses, freckles, and blonde hair, the girl was in the same engineering program as Kate, and they'd gotten the internship together. Both would have to arrive at 5:00 in the morning each Tuesday for the next eight weeks. It was just the second week and Kate was already hating the early hour.

"Rough everything," she said.

"Are things not going well with Reed?"

Kate smiled softly. "Great, actually."

Sara shook her head, making her ponytail dance. "I still can't believe he hijacked your date."

"He's unlike anyone I've ever met."

"Sounds like you're in love."

This time Kate kept her smile on the inside. "We're just having a good time together."

Sara grunted, the sound reflecting a world of doubt. She rolled her chair out of her cubicle and into Kate's. Then she folded her arms and waited. Kate smiled and turned her computer on, but Sara continued to wait.

"I don't know where it's going," Kate said honestly. "I just know I'm having fun."

"Then what's with the groan?"

"Our challenge has gotten out of hand," Kate said. "It started small, but now it seems like everyone is involved. Every time I talk to my mother she gushes about Reed, and I never know if I can trust my roommates. We were up till one last night arguing about my next date and I kept wondering how much they were going to tell him."

Sara's expression turned guilty. "We're still your friends."

Kate heard the *we* and her eyes narrowed. "What do you know?"

"Nothing," Sara said. She attempted to roll away but Kate's hand shot out and grabbed her chair.

"What do you know?" Kate repeated sharply.

Sara's eyes sought for escape but there was none. They were the only ones on the floor this early, and the darkened offices and cubicles offered no salvation. Grimacing, Sara shook her head.

"I know I'm supposed to give you a ride home from work today."

"Why will I need a ride?"

"I don't know," she said. "Honestly, I just know you're going to need a ride."

Pleased she'd managed to get some information, Kate released Sara's chair and leaned back. "At least I know he's going to ask today."

"He's really cute, you know."

"You met him?" she asked, surprised.

"He caught me when I left work last Tuesday," Sara admitted. "Asked for my help. How could I refuse such a romantic?"

"You can't," she said, half disparaging, half admiring.

Sara shook her head. "We all dream of meeting a guy like that and you meet him on a blind date. How do I get mine?"

Kate laughed lightly. "I don't know if he's even mine yet."

"But you want him to be?"

Kate didn't hesitate. "Of course."

"Then what are you waiting for?"

"Him," she said. "He feels the same for me, I can tell, but something is holding him back."

"You think he's lying to you?"

Kate shook her head. "Why would he? He hasn't even touched me. Usually guys lie because they want sex."

"Or they lie because they have something to hide."

"True," Kate agreed. "But I don't get the feeling he did anything wrong. I think regret drives him to date the way he does."

"So what does that mean for you?" Sara asked, leaning back in her chair. "Can you be with him if he has a secret like that?"

"You think he'll never tell me?" she asked. She hadn't considered that possibility.

"Everyone has secrets," Sara said. "The question isn't *if* they have them, it's if you can live with them."

Kate considered her words until a door clicked open and one of the other assistant engineers entered. Yawning, the man strode to his office. The key clicked in the lock and then he shuffled out of sight. Sara gave Kate a searching look and then returned to her cubicle.

Sara was always smart, both with people and with math. She wasn't what most guys would consider pretty, making her prospects limited. In fact, she was exactly the type of girl Reed might have taken on a date. When she'd talked about finding a guy like Reed, her eyes had been wistful, a yearning that bordered on desperation.

Is that what Reed saw? Is that why he dated as he did? She frowned, wondering if she could live with his secret, wondering if he would ever reveal it. Although Reed was an open book with everything else, he had yet to reveal his motivations.

Throughout the day she struggled to focus on work, but her thoughts were dominated by the ramifications of Sara's comments. Kate wanted to dismiss them but couldn't, and by 2:00 pm she'd realized that as much as she felt for Reed, if he couldn't reveal what held him back, she couldn't stay with him.

The certainty was sobering, and she realized their dates had been progressively more serious, exemplified by his kissing her cheek. Like two trains racing towards each other on the same track, they were bound for a collision.

Sara appeared promptly at two. "Ready?" she asked, her tone betraying her eagerness.

"Ready," Kate said.

She gathered her purse and rose to her feet. Although she'd been conflicted all day, a sense of certainty permeated her thoughts. She knew what she wanted, and knew she could no longer wait.

As they walked to the elevator, Sara was jittery. Several times she'd looked out the window in an attempt to see Kate's car but Kate had parked around the corner. They entered the elevator and Sara stabbed the button.

"How are you not more excited?" she asked.

"I am excited," Kate said honestly, a flicker of anticipation sparking in her heart. "With Reed, everything is exciting."

"Does he have a brother?" she asked.

"Only a sister," Kate replied.

"Why are all the good ones taken?" Sara lamented.

Kate caught her eye. "We only say that until we find a good one."

The elevator pinged and they walked out of the building together. "You really think there's one for me?" Sara asked, her tone doubtful.

"Everyone has their match," Kate said.

Sara raised an eyebrow. "Does that mean you're his match?"

45

They came to a halt facing Kate's car. "I don't know about that," Kate breathed.

The parking lot had transformed while they were at work. Black paper and cardboard covered her car, making it look like a mine cart. Mine tracks stretched away from the wheels and entered a cave, also built from cardboard and wood. The theatre-level display transformed the corner of the parking lot into a gold mine, complete with glittering gold nuggets glimmering in the walls.

"It just appeared," a woman said to Sara, her voice awed as she took pictures. "I was out here an hour ago and it wasn't here."

The mine was quickly drawing a crowd, with dozens already gathered around, taking pictures and video. Sara spotted a chest hidden next to Kate's car-turned-minecart. With the lid cracked open and light spilling from the interior, it begged to be explored.

"Well?" Sara demanded. "If you don't open it, I will."

Kate grinned and strode to the chest, drawing a shout from the swelling crowd that realized it was for her. She stooped to the chest and lifted the lid to find a map and a letter. She pulled it open and, at the urging of her colleagues, read aloud.

"To a girl with a heart of gold, you deserve an adventure. I'll take you to a mine of old, to a world of depth and treasure."

She smiled and swept her hand at the crowd. "It appears I have a date," she called.

One Reed was not prepared for.

Chapter 2

After enduring endless pictures by her work friends, Kate abandoned her car and rode home with Sara, who gushed about Reed's romantic invitation. As they pulled into the driveway she shook her head.

"If a guy did that for me I would do *anything* for him," she said.

"That's not what he wants," Kate said.

Sara put her car into park. "Then what does he want?"

"I intend to find out."

Sara raised an eyebrow. "Oh?"

"I'll let you know after the date," she said.

"I'll be waiting," Sara said.

Kate grinned and exited the car. Waving to Sara, she made her way to the door and unlocked it, stepping inside to find the house empty. As she walked to her room she pulled out her phone and typed a quick text.

My car was vandalized. Do you think I should report it?

Reed's response was quick. **Savages.**

Kate giggled as she put her purse down and flopped onto her bed. **Seriously. How did you set it up so quickly?**

We built it in pieces so it would be easier to put together, he replied, and then a moment later added, **If it had taken too long you would have caught the setup before it was finished. Couldn't have that, could we?**

I take it we're going to a mine?

Fair guess, he messaged. **But there are a few surprises in store.**

She smiled and said aloud, "For you as well."

Why Saturday instead of Thursday? she asked.

The location is a little far, so Saturday works better. You don't mind spending a few extra hours with me?

I'll move a few things around. She said.

Then I'll pick you up at 10:00

Looking forward to it.

She smiled and put her phone down. Her bed was soft on her back, her pillow cradling her head. After the short night and the long day, fatigue overpowered her and she drifted off to slumber. She dreamed of Reed and exploring a mine, of what they would do when they were alone in the dark . . .

When she woke it was already night, and she rubbed her eyes as she sat up, surprised to find how long she'd slept. She left her room to find Ember and Brittney sitting on the couch, both doing homework. They looked up at Kate's entrance.

"About time you woke up," Ember said. "Don't you have homework to do?"

"It's the first week of classes," Kate said, sinking into a chair.

"Dr. Kendric didn't get the memo," Ember said acidly. "I'm supposed to read four chapters by Monday morning, and I'm going out of town this weekend."

"Where to?" Kate asked, stifling a yawn.

"Remember Simmons on the basketball team?" Brittney asked.

Kate vaguely recalled he was one of Jackson's friends. "The dark haired one?"

Brittney smirked and stabbed a finger at Ember. "Ember asked him out."

48

"Really?" Kate asked.

"Don't sound so surprised," Ember said. "You can't have all the fun."

"What about the chess club guy?" Kate asked.

"Still in the picture," Ember said. "We are sort of dating, but he wants to take it slow—too slow. Which is why I'm taking Simmons on a date."

"She hopes to make him jealous," Brittney said.

"It's a fair tactic," Ember said.

"Perhaps I should hijack your date," Kate mused.

Brittney laughed while Ember glowered. "Are you ever going to let that go?"

"When you promise not to interfere like that again," Kate said.

"Can't a girl look out for her roommates?" Ember asked.

"You did take it a bit far," Brittney said.

Ember rounded on her. "You said it was the only way he would ever kiss her."

Brittney flushed, but before Ember could do any more damage Kate raised her hand. "While I'm grateful for the push, I'd like to handle it from here."

Both girls turned to stare at her, and Ember's eyes turned calculating. "You have a plan," she accused.

"I do," Kate said. "And I need you to trust me. You can help him when he asks, but no more inserting your own agenda. Agreed?"

They exchanged a look and Brittney nodded. "I promise."

Ember regarded Kate for several seconds until retreating with a muttered, "Fine. But I reserve the right to say I told you so when he doesn't kiss you."

"Deal," Kate said, grateful for the ground she'd gained. "Now what's for dinner?"

Brittney perked up. "Cornbread waffles?"

"Sounds delicious," Kate said.

Brittney set about cooking dinner and Kate joined her. As they bustled about the kitchen the door opened and closed, and Marta dropped her pack on the floor before taking Brittney's seat with a sigh.

"Please tell me I smell cornbread waffles," she called.

"With cheese and chili," Brittney called back.

"Who needs a man when you have Brittney's food?" she asked.

They sat down to eat and for the next several minutes talked about school, Reed, work, and everything in between. As they talked Kate realized that the initial euphoria of Reed's creative dating had worn off, and it had become normal. They still giggled and talked about the pictures of her minecart car, but it was not with the same spark of shock the initial dates had inspired.

She recalled something Reed had said recently, that guys could not pretend to be someone they were not, at least not for long. She'd wondered then how long one had to wait before a guy showed his true colors, and suspected that she'd crossed the threshold in recent weeks.

She marveled at the change in her roommates. Prior to Reed's appearance most meals were spent talking about work, school, and guys. When one of the girls had spent the night at a guy's house they would talk about it for weeks, wondering where the relationship would go. Now Kate could not recall the last time they'd had such a conversation.

Ember, by far the one most likely to spend the night out, hadn't done so in weeks, and her conversation had shifted. Instead of lamenting the dogs she dated, she'd elevated her standards, and now seemed intent on finding a "keeper."

Had Reed influenced them all? Perhaps they'd just seen what Kate and Reed shared and wanted it, instinctively realizing that it required a different sort of perspective. Kate smiled as she realized her own perspective on dating had forever been altered.

"What's that smile for?" Marta asked, leaning back and sipping her beer.

"Just thinking about what Reed has done to us," Kate said.

"To us?" Brittney asked, taking the last bite from her plate.

"When's the last time Ember spent the night at a guy's house?" Kate asked. "Or Brittney complaining when guys don't ask her out?"

"I asked one out last week . . . oh." Brittney smiled. "I see what you mean."

"I don't," Ember said with a frown.

"He's changing how we view men," Marta said.

Ember snorted in disagreement. "They're still dogs."

"True," Kate said with a laugh. "But you now think you can find a good one, don't you?"

Ember scowled. "Attributing my attitude to Reed is a bit of a stretch. I'm not the one dating him."

"I'm just wondering if he's right," Kate said with a shrug. "Maybe we do date wrong."

Ember grunted in irritation and stood. "His method works for him. Doesn't mean it will work for everyone. Guys won't call. They won't show respect. And they will continue to rape and assault women."

Her voice rose with heat, surprising Kate with the sudden shift in conversation. "I'm sorry," Kate said hastily. "I was just wondering out loud."

"Well don't," Ember said.

She picked up her plate and dropped it into the sink with a clatter. Then she stomped to her room and all but slammed the door. In the ensuing quiet Kate shook her head. Ember always ran hot, but the outburst was uncharacteristic in their home. Then Brittney sighed and lowered her tone.

"Remember when Gavin asked her out?"

Kate recalled Ember talking about him a few weeks ago. "Did it not end well?"

"She caught him trying to drug her drink," Brittney said.

"I bet she went nuclear," Marta said with a grimace.

"She broke his jaw," Brittney said.

"Why didn't she tell us?" Kate asked.

Brittney's eyes settled on her. "She didn't want to interrupt what you have going on with Reed. She won't admit it, but it's given her hope that she can find someone. But Gavin almost broke that hope."

Kate groaned and made to stand, but Marta caught her arm. "Let her calm down. Then talk to her. We all know she doesn't respond well when she's that angry."

Kate slowly sank back into her chair and shuddered. "I can't believe he tried to rape her."

"We've all been there," Marta said. "Some closer than others. It's the world we live in."

"Doesn't mean it's okay," Kate said, and thought of all her close calls.

"We don't all have Ember's anger to defend us," Brittney said quietly.

"You mean you . . .?"

Brittney nodded and began to clear off the table. The quiet was deafening, but Kate stood and wrapped her arms around her friend. Marta joined her, and together they simply held Brittney.

Chapter 3

In the days leading up to Kate's date with Reed, she found herself anxious. As had become normal, they continued to text and talk on the phone, but for the first time she avoided interaction, claiming distractions from her first week of summer semester. The desire to confront Reed burgeoned within her, but she didn't want to have such a conversation over the phone.

"Or text," Ember agreed emphatically when Kate voiced her thoughts over Saturday's breakfast. "Breaking up over text is really stupid."

"She's not breaking up," Brittney said, and then her eyes flicked to Kate. "Are you?"

Kate's gut clenched. "I hope not," she said fervently.

"He'll be here soon," Brittney said. "You should get ready."

She sighed and went to her bedroom. Discarding several outfits, she settled on jeans and a t-shirt. Reed had informed her that going into a mine could get dirty, so she chose clothes that wouldn't mind a stain. It was raining, so she grabbed a jacket as well.

She went back and sat on the couch, trying not to fidget as she watched the documentary Brittney was viewing for her class. Reed arrived shortly before ten and knocked on the door, and she jumped, surprised even though it was expected.

She stepped to the door and swung it open. Dressed in a pair of well-worn jeans and a Batman T-shirt, he also wore a jacket to ward off the rain, which sluiced into the street in quiet sheets. His hair was wet and dripped onto his jacket, which glistened with moisture.

"Ready?" he asked.

"Ready," she said, casting a look at her roommates.

"Good luck!" Ember called, and Brittney echoed the statement.

Reed flipped an umbrella up and walked her to the car. Although it was June, the rain carried a chill that made Kate shiver. It should have been bright and shiny, but the ominous clouds made the late morning feel like nightfall.

"Is there something I should know?" Reed asked as he held the door and umbrella for her.

"Why do you ask?"

"Just the way your roommates wished you luck," he said. "Just seemed like they meant more."

She smiled and shook her head, but didn't trust herself to speak. His eyes betrayed a hint of doubt, but he shut the door and made his way around the car. Water ushered him in as he closed the umbrella and stowed it behind his seat.

"You said you've never been to a mine?"

"I've explored caves before," she said as they backed into the street, "but never a mine."

He smiled. "We've got about an hour and a half to get there. Then they'll take us 600 feet down. We'll even get to do a little mining of our own on the gold vein."

"Really?" she asked.

She wondered how much gold it took to make a wedding ring. She stifled the thought and listened to him explain the mine and the activity as he left Boulder behind and pulled onto a smaller highway.

The rain picked up as they headed west, taking Highway 119 as it wound through the mountains. Trees interspersed open fields and scattered homes, the settlements growing more distant as they worked their way toward Tungsten Mountain.

"Have you ever been camping out here?" she asked.

He shook his head. "Jackson and I have taken a few trips to the Greenbelt Plateau, but never this direction. You?"

"I miss camping," she said, watching the rain soak a field, the image reminding her of another field. "Before my dad left we would go camping at a place called Wildhorse Creek. We'd catch trout for dinner and hike up to Boulder Lake.

"One year it rained most of the week and the tarp over the fire sagged, the water collecting into a big bubble. Bake decided to push it up and drain the water, but my dad was standing too close and it dumped all over both of them. I've never heard my dad swear so much, but we were all laughing."

"Sounds like a place worth visiting," Reed said, meeting her gaze before returning his attention to the road.

"I haven't been back since my dad left," she said. "But I'd like to."

"Am I hearing your next date?" he asked.

"An overnight camping trip?" she asked. "Doesn't that push your rules a little bit?"

"We'll use separate tents," he said, nodding like it was settled.

"Camping with my non-boyfriend in separate tents. What has my life become?"

They shared a laugh, but Reed glanced her way again, his eyes filled with curiosity. Realizing she might have given too much of her thoughts away with the boyfriend comment, she pointed to a passing cabin.

"Would you rather live in the city or the country?"

"Between the two," he said.

"Like a suburb?"

"Like the outskirts of a city," he corrected. "I'd like it quiet but not have to drive an hour to get to the grocery store. You?"

"City, I guess, but I've never lived in the country, so I can't really compare."

"I used to live in a trailer park in the woods," he said.

"Really?" she swiveled to look at him.

"No," he said with a laugh.

She slapped his arm in mock anger. "Liar."

"One summer, I did live in a cabin with my grandfather," he said. "It wasn't a trailer, but it wasn't large either. I cut wood and went fishing most days, and helped him in his garden. My sister and I stayed there while my parents worked out their divorce. When we came home there were two of everything, two cars, two houses, two Thanksgivings."

"I hated that part," she said. "No one needs that much turkey."

"Have you ever taken a boyfriend home for a holiday?" he asked.

She threw him a sharp look, but he was focused on the road as a truck passed them, showering the car with water. The rain picked up, splattering the roof of the car, forcing them to talk loud in order to be heard. She suspected that bringing up a boyfriend was his attempt to fish about the topic, but without looking at his eyes she couldn't be sure.

"Jason, once," she said. "My brothers said they liked them. Then he left and they said they hated him."

Reed snorted. "Sounds like a fast reversal."

"It was," she said. "They liked the whole doctor aspect, but I think I told you his nickname."

"Nappy," he said with a nod. "I remember. Should I worry about what they'll call me?"

"Oh, you already have a nickname," she said with a sly smile. "Bake decided to call you Valentine."

"Because of our first date?"

56

"Because you're a romantic," she said.

He laughed lightly. "I suppose it could have been worse."

Abruptly the car shuddered and slowed, the engine beginning to labor. Reed frowned and gently tapped the gas, but nothing happened. The engine chugged like a dying animal gasping for breath, their momentum only holding as they coasted down an incline. The old Camry struggled, but the lights dimmed and they slowed when the incline leveled off. Reed's frown turned into a scowl as he pulled onto the shoulder, where the car promptly died.

"It's not overheating," he said, trying to start the car again, but the starter merely whined its futility.

"I suppose it just got worse," she said with a smile.

He laughed and turned to face her. "I could pop the hood and pretend to look at the engine, but it would be about as useful as trying to push."

She laughed and pulled out her phone, her smile fading as she realized she had no signal. "Too far out," she said.

He checked his phone, and for the first time a trace of worry appeared in his voice. "Me too," he said.

Their eyes met and it was clear they were thinking the same thing. The car had died an hour outside of Boulder and they couldn't call for help. They were trapped, and the storm was still mounting.

Chapter 4

"Is this part of the date?" she asked nervously.

"I wish I could say it is," he said, still trying his phone. "But sadly, it's just my car deciding to quit on the job."

"At least there's one benefit from this," she said.

"What's that?"

"I *totally* win this round."

He grunted in disagreement. "You're going to take a win because my car broke down?"

"Wouldn't you?"

"No," he said. "Probably. Okay, I would—but you haven't seen how I handle it yet."

She folded her arms and raised an eyebrow. He laughed at her silent challenge and reached for the umbrella. As he prepared to exit he popped the trunk and pointed to the rain, which came down in sheets across the road and countryside.

"The forecast this morning said the rain would lighten up this afternoon. Unless you want to go trudging through the mud, I suggest we hunker down here and have lunch, and then find a nearby house."

"How romantic."

He grinned. "I'll be back."

He opened the door and rain assaulted her. Even with the umbrella he was pummeled as he went to the trunk. A moment later he returned with his legs drenched. Shivering, he shut the door and shook his wet hair. Then he handed the old backpack to her.

"Hungry?"

"What's this?" she asked.

"It's my emergency kit," he said.

"You actually have one?"

"Last fall Shelby watched a documentary called 'Stranded' on the nature channel. She made Jackson and I make emergency kits. She's going to love it when I tell her she was right."

"Please tell me you have something tasty."

He raised his hands helplessly. "I honestly don't remember. It's as much a surprise for me as it is for you."

She laughed and unzipped the bag. She began pulling everything out, surprised to find it fairly well stocked. Nuts, beef jerky, and a few cans of peaches were packed with Cup-o-Noodle, beef flavor. A few bottles of water were stacked neatly in the bottom.

"I'll have to thank Shelby," she said, opening a bag of peanuts.

He reached over and opened a smaller pocket which held a can opener, and began opening a can of peaches. "I thought she was a little paranoid, but we grabbed whatever we could find in the cupboards and loaded old backpacks. Jackson slipped a bottle of scotch into his pack when Shelby wasn't looking."

"What are we supposed to do with the Cup-O-Noodle?" she asked, holding one up.

Reed shrugged. "I didn't really think it through."

"We could use the cigarette lighter to warm water," she said. "But it won't work in a water bottle."

"How about the can?" he replied, raising the opened can of peaches for emphasis. "Peaches are the first course, noodles are the second."

They set to work preparing a makeshift meal. Heating a can of water on a cigarette lighter proved to be a challenge, but working together they managed to heat water sufficiently to add to the noodles.

"This is the strangest date I've been on," she said, taking a bite. There was only one fork, so she then passed it to him. "But it's delicious."

He slurped a noodle. "Am I gaining points for spontaneity?"

"Yes," she said. "But not enough to make up for the car dying."

He grinned and used the plastic fork to gesture to the car. "It's got 240,000 miles on it. I'd say the car has lived a long life."

"So, are you going to put it out of its misery?"

"Shh," Reed admonished, passing the fork back to her. "I don't want her to know I'm sending her to a farm to retire."

"Trading her in?"

"I've saved up a few thousand," he replied. "I want a nice, cheap, newer model."

She burst into a laugh. "You're trading your car in for a newer version? Will it have a nice body?"

"Hopefully," he said. "But I'm more concerned about the engine. It's what's inside that counts."

"That's what all guys say," she lamented. "But they all want the body."

He smiled and shook his head. "Not all."

She inclined her head, conceding the point, but her thoughts shifted to Ember. Kate hadn't talked to her about Gavin, and Ember had pretended her anger had never happened. With Ember it was impossible to know if she really was upset or if she'd let it go.

"Is something wrong?" he asked.

She hesitated, and then shared what had happened to Ember. When she finished his expression had darkened. She sipped her now lukewarm noodles, surprised to see anger tighten his features. She'd never seen him angry.

"Is she okay?" he asked.

"I'm not sure," she said. "With Ember, most emotions turn into anger at some point. But with this? I think she's still hurting."

"I hate how men think they can do that," he said, stabbing at his food with the fork.

"At least you're different," she said. "And whether you've intended to or not, my roommates and I now have hope that there are still decent guys out there."

"Too few," he said bitterly.

"Maybe," she said, wondering why the story had elicited such a strong reaction. "But I hope the others can change."

He put his cup down and shook his head. "I have a friend doing a thesis similar to mine, except his is on male dating behavior. With apps like Tinder and websites devoted to cheating husbands, he wanted to see if there was a correlation between how men date and men that cheat."

"Is there?"

"He hasn't found one yet," he said.

"Is there a correlation to the good ones?" she asked. "Inquiring minds want to know."

"All I can say is that time tends to increase affection," he said. "But that assumes there is already affection to enhance."

"How many dates does it take to fall in love?"

"That depends on how much affection there was to start," he said, his anger gradually fading from his voice.

"Let's say a lot," she said, and then smiled. "For argument's sake."

"Then not long," he said, his lips twitching with amusement. "But that assumes there are no other factors that impact the relationship."

"Like what?"

"Like an ex reappearing."

She held his gaze. "And what if the ex is gone? Then how many dates?"

"For two people to fall in love?" He scrunched his face up and muttered numbers like he was solving a math problem. "One day."

"That's it?" she asked. "I think your math is off."

"I didn't say the first day," Reed said. "It could be the tenth day, or a day in the second year. But all it takes is one day."

"So how do you know which day counts?"

"How should I know?" he said. "My thesis doesn't cover everything—and my premise could be entirely wrong."

"I hope not," she said fervently.

He smiled and motioned to the rain, which had diminished enough the region was not obscured. A short distance ahead a driveway led off the road, and through the trees Kate spotted a house nested in the trees at the edge of a farm.

"Looks like the rain is letting up," he said. "Ready to get out of here?"

"No," she said. "It's cozy in here."

"In my broken down car?"

"It's comfortable," she said, disliking the idea of walking in the rain.

"You can stay here if you'd like," he said. "I'll come back once I talk to them."

"And if no one is home?"

"Then I'll go to the next house to call Jackson," he said. "He won't mind coming to pick us up. I hope."

He'd begun to gather the garbage up. She added hers, and smiled to herself as she put the single fork into the trash. She'd shared it without thinking, as if they were an old married couple and they shared everything.

"I'm going with you," she decided.

"Are you sure?" he asked as lightning flashed nearby. "You just said it's comfortable in the car."

"That's because you're here," she said.

He grinned. "Let's find out if farmer Joe is friendly."

Chapter 5

Kate stepped out of the car and ducked under the umbrella. The rain had slowed to a drizzle but the wind still carried a chill, causing her to shiver. Pressed against each other under the umbrella, they hiked to the driveway and started towards the house.

"Just how long is the driveway?" Reed asked.

"Too long," she said.

They rounded a curve and ascended to the house, which proved to be a two-story structure with a wraparound porch. A barn was visible beyond the house, as well as a pair of sheds. A battered truck sat in the driveway, rain washing at the rust.

They walked up the path to the house, the boards of the porch creaking as they climbed the steps. Reed collapsed the umbrella while Kate knocked on the door. It didn't take long before the inside door swung open and a tiny, white-haired woman appeared. She took one look at them freezing on the porch and ushered them inside.

"You'll catch your death of cold," she scolded, and then turned toward the living room, where the sounds of a television rumbled. "HAROLD!" she shouted with surprising vigor. "Get some towels!"

A chair creaked and a large man appeared in the hall. With more hair on his chin than his head, he looked them up and down and then turned away, rumbling a, "yes, dear," as he walked out of view. A moment later the giant returned with two towels.

"I'm Marge," the woman said, "but everyone calls me Pepper."

"Our car broke down up the road," Reed said, drying his hair. "We were hoping to use your phone."

"Of course," she said. "Are you hungry? HAROLD! Go look at their car!"

"Yes, dear."

A back door opened and shut before Reed could argue. "He doesn't need to do anything," he said. "My roommate will come and get us and I'll call a mechanic."

"Harold knows his way around an engine," she said with a high laugh, shooing them into the kitchen. "Do you need a shower to warm up?"

"We're fine," Kate said, introducing herself to the woman. Reed did as well.

"Reed and Kate," Marge said, nodding to them. "You make a beautiful couple. Now sit down so I can make you some food."

Reed and Kate exchanged a look, but neither challenged her assumption. The effort would probably be futile, because she continued to chatter as she stepped into the kitchen and set to work. Reed grinned and took a seat at the table.

The entranceway led to the living room and dining area, which contained piles of newspapers and books across the table and chairs. Faded pictures of children and grandchildren covered the walls, and little glass mementos sat in a cabinet. The whole house smelled of warm bread, and Kate breathed deep.

"It smells wonderful," she called.

"Bread's almost out of the oven," Pepper called back. "Do you prefer jam or cinnamon? Never mind, I'll bring both."

"Is she really going to feed us?" Kate whispered.

"I don't think we can say no," Reed said with a smile.

The clatter of the oven door preceded the sound of three bread pans being set on the stove. A moment later she came with a steaming loaf resting on a cutting board. She returned a moment later with a knife and a pair of plates, and again with milk and cups.

"Hot bread makes everything better," she said, expertly slicing the bread and putting a generous portion on each plate.

"Your hospitality is quickly becoming legendary," Reed said with a smile.

Pepper's smile was as warm as the bread. "Harold will be back any moment."

"I really can call a mechanic," Reed said.

"Don't be silly, dear," she said with an airy wave.

The back door opened and shut and Harold appeared in the doorway. "Fuel pump," he said simply. "Carl's on his way with a new one."

"You're fixing my car?" Reed asked.

Harold grunted, the sound bordering on amusement, before he left again. Reed half stood, calling out, "I can help . . ."

"Nonsense," Pepper said, all but pushing him back into his seat. "You two eat."

Reed shook his head in disbelief and looked to Kate, who shrugged in amusement. Realizing Pepper would not be dissuaded, he took a bite of the bread, his expression proving it to be delicious. He gestured to an empty seat.

"Are you joining us . . ." But Pepper was at the back door, putting on her raincoat.

"I'll just make sure he's doing it right," Pepper said. "I'll be back shortly."

The door clattered shut, leaving them in the house by themselves. They both laughed quietly and ate the bread. Kate was careful not to burn herself as she ate, the bread a perfect end to their spontaneous meal in the car. When they finished, Reed gestured to the porch.

"I feel weird sitting in their house."

"Agreed," she said, relieved he'd said it.

They cleared their plates and set them in the sink, and then returned to the front porch. Neither Pepper nor Harold was in sight, so they sat on the rocking chairs close to the front window.

The rain had all but stopped, but a sprinkling continued to wet the air. Although more dark clouds loomed in the distance, the sun momentarily peeked through, warming the air and glistening off the moisture.

"This is beautiful," Kate murmured.

"Are you changing your answer from city?" he asked.

"I think I am," she said.

They were silent for a moment, with both enjoying the atmosphere. Kate noticed Reed glancing her way but thought nothing of it. Then he shifted his chair and waited until she turned and raised an eyebrow.

"Are you going to tell me what's weighing on your mind?" he asked.

"Sometimes I forget how well you read me."

He smiled. "Only because I've spent so much time with you."

She watched the clouds part and sunshine fall on the trees, taking a moment to gather her thoughts. Nervous, she struggled to form the words she'd been framing for the last few weeks, surprised to find them difficult to voice.

"What are we to each other?"

"I'm not sure what you're asking."

She turned and settled her gaze on him. "We're more than friends, that much is clear. But we aren't dating either."

He looked away. "You know the rules."

"I want to change them."

He turned back to face her. "How so?"

She leaned forward, trying unsuccessfully not to fidget. "I know there is something holding you back, and you don't have to share it—at least not yet. But I think we both know where we are headed. I just want to stop pretending."

He regarded her with a strained expression. "I care for you a great deal," he admitted. "But I can't do what you're asking."

"I'm not asking," she said. "I'm telling you. My feelings for you keep getting deeper with every text, call, and especially every date. I broke up with Jason because we didn't have what you and I have. I don't have a name for it. I can't define it. I just know that I want it."

"What exactly are you saying?" he asked.

She gathered her courage. "I'm not going to wait forever."

He settled back in his chair and seemed to stare miles past her. She held her breath, hoping, praying, he wouldn't say it was over. She'd said what she felt but not the depth of her feelings. Even after the dates they'd gone on, she wasn't certain she could trust him that much. Not yet.

"I don't know if I can do what you want," he said softly.

"Then we can part ways," she said, struggling to contain the sudden burst of fear.

"Will you give me time to think about it?"

Relief flooded her frame, so palpable she could taste its warmth. "I don't want to stop dating you, Reed. But if your rules don't change, I will."

"I understand," he said.

Recognizing the conversation had reached an end, she rotated her chair and tried not to let her anxiety show on her face. They sat in silence, watching the rain gradually pick up again, as if the clouds had parted to bring a moment of clarity to just them. Shortly after, Harold and Pepper appeared at the end of the driveway.

He carried a tool bag while she carried a dark piece of machinery. Kate smiled when she saw their hands intertwined. Both dressed in rain slickers, they walked up the porch steps and Pepper removed her hat.

"Your car is ready to go," she said.

Reed was already on his feet. "Thank you," he said. "How much do I owe you?"

"The part cost—"

"Harold," Pepper said sharply.

"Yes, dear," he rumbled. "Take care of your girl, there."

Harold stepped off the porch and walked toward the barn. Kate wasn't sure if he'd been talking about her or Reed's car, but Pepper was all smiles. She removed her hat and shook her white hair. Then she smiled and gestured inside.

"You're welcome to stay a while. The storm's picking up again."

"No, thank you," Reed said. "We'd better get back."

"The bread was delicious," Kate said, and impulsively hugged the woman.

"Well thank you, dear," she said, her tone pleased. "Stop in anytime."

Reed stepped forward and embraced her as well. "That was for Harold," he said.

She laughed lightly. "I'll make sure he gets the message."

He picked up the umbrella and opened it, and Kate stepped beneath its protection. As they strode to the car it seemed to her that Reed walked a fraction apart, yet a chasm had appeared between them.

Chapter 6

They got into the car and Reed turned around, obviously headed back to Boulder. Kate assumed it was because of the delay, not because of their conversation. She hoped. She assumed. She hoped. She frowned and looked out the window.

"Can I ask you a question?" Reed asked.

"What type of question?"

"How much time?" She glanced his way and saw cautious amusement on his features. When their eyes met he broke into a tentative smile. "I mean, today? Next week? A few months?"

"You want an actual deadline?" she asked, unable to resist his smile.

"That would be helpful," he said.

She considered an answer and then shrugged. "Two months," she said.

"Good," he said, his tone relieved.

She waited for him to explain and when he didn't she asked, "Why?"

"Because I've already planned our next date," he said. "And I'm not taking another girl."

"I should hope not," she said.

They both laughed, the humor easing the tension. The conversation shifted to other topics, but Kate frequently found his eyes on her, and knew he was thinking about her ultimatum. Content to wait, she did not bring it up again.

"I wish we could go to the mine," she lamented.

"Some other time," he said. "Our tour is over by now so I'll have to reschedule."

"For a spontaneous date, it ended up ranking fairly well," she said. "Better than dates with other guys, but not your best."

"You're not going to let me live it down, are you."

She smiled and rubbed her hands together like a villain. "Nope. Now I get to take the lead."

"You think so?"

"And I know just what to do," she said.

He released an exaggerated sigh. "I guess I have to let you win *one* round."

"*Let* me win?" She smacked him on the shoulder. "I don't think so. Harold and Pepper may have improved your date, but it was still a bust."

"Oh, that reminds me," he said, pointing to the glove compartment. "Can you grab a pen and paper?"

"Why?" she asked, doing as he requested.

"I want you to write down their address."

"You know it?"

"I spotted it on the mail on the table," he said. "I want to send them money for the fuel pump."

"They won't accept that," she said.

"I know," he said, and smiled. "That's why I'm going to say its payment for the bread."

She grinned and scribbled down the address. Then she put the pen away and placed the notepad on the dash. The gesture was clever and thoughtful, and Kate realized that Reed's flair for the creative went beyond dating.

They talked and laughed the rest of the way home, but Kate felt the omnipresent weight of her ultimatum. It didn't wear on her shoulders—instead, it seemed to make every conversation more real. A gauntlet had been thrown down, and the challenge would either be accepted . . . or rejected.

With a distant deadline, she found herself feeling confident, but a seed of doubt lodged in her gut. Losing Jason had cost her a year of regret. What would be the price of losing Reed? She shuddered and watched the rain fall, fighting to put her doubt back into its corner.

They reached her house and he walked her to the door, reaching it just as the storm picked up again, the rain battering his car, the house, and the lawn. Side spray drifted across them, the air growing chilly once again.

"Your turn," he said, pulling her into an embrace.

"See you soon," she said.

Heat blossomed in her chest as she clung to him. The seconds passed and she kept waiting for him to speak or pull away. He did neither. When he finally did, his voice was barely audible over the storm.

"Whatever happens," he murmured, "I feel the same as you."

Then he pulled away and sprinted to his car, ducking into the driver's seat as she stood on the porch. The freezing air battered her frame, intent on sapping every shred of heat. But she was no longer cold. Her heart beat against her ribs, sending heat flooding her frame, burning all the way into her toes.

He hadn't said he was falling for her.

But that's what she'd heard.

Volume 10: The Race Date

Chapter 1

"You have to tell her," Jackson said.

"I can't," Reed said. "She won't understand."

"If you don't tell her, you'll lose her anyway," Jackson said.

They were sitting at the kitchen table. It had been several hours since his failed date with Kate, but the storm still raged, the rain falling in sheets that clattered off the roof. Jackson had walked in at eight and found Reed sitting on the couch, staring at a dark screen. At his prompting, Reed had shared Kate's ultimatum.

Jackson stepped to the fridge and returned with two beers and a soda for Reed. Then he sank into his seat and stared out the window in the backyard. Time slipped by as they both watched the rain.

"I don't want to lose her," Reed said, gripping the cold can in his hand.

"Then you have to break your promise to Aura," Jackson said.

Reed released a long breath. "That promise has become everything."

"I know," Jackson said. "But which do you want more, a promise from the past? Or the promise of a future?"

Reed raised an eyebrow to his roommate. "Since when do you have poignant advice?"

"I'm not just a sports guy," Jackson said, his tone indignant.

"Are you sure you didn't read it on a fortune cookie?"

Jackson grinned. "Quote of the day, actually."

Reed laughed, his amusement fading as thunder rumbled in the distance. As they continued to talk he reminded himself that he had a few weeks, and it was her turn to ask him out. They continued to debate his predicament until the dropping temperatures drove them inside.

Abruptly tired, Reed got ready for bed and then wrote a note to Harold and Pepper that included the money for the fuel pump. Distracted as he was, he didn't want to forget. When he was finished he fished through his desk until he found a stamp and left it ready on his desk. Then he climbed into bed with his phone.

I enjoyed today, he sent to Kate.

Her response came quickly. **So did I. But I was afraid of your response.**

Why?

Because I didn't know what you felt. Our challenge is fun, but we don't really talk about those kinds of things.

Reed hesitated, and then said, **I don't want our challenge to end.**

I'm ready to listen when you're ready to talk.

I know. He said.

Reed waited for a response but none came, so he plugged his phone in and then put his head down. He watched the phone, hoping for another text, but the next thing he knew his alarm blared for him to wake up.

Over the next week he cancelled the only two dates not with Kate. He'd already stopped planning new ones because it wouldn't be fair to another girl. It did mean he was only dating Kate, but they hadn't advanced their relationship, so it wasn't technically exclusive. He hoped.

A week after his date, he sat back and stared at his wall calendar of the year. Just four months ago it had been packed with dates, sometimes four in a week. Now his schedule just showed Kate's name scribbled in. Although the calendar was open, it didn't feel empty.

He stepped out of his room and shouldered his backpack just as Jackson appeared in his door, also shouldering his backpack. They shared a grin and stepped to the door together. Reed swung the front door open to reveal a bright sunrise cresting over the homes across the street.

"Looks like a nice day . . ."

Reed trailed off as he caught sight of his car. He'd parked it the previous night in its usual spot, right next to Jackson's truck. Although it was obviously still his car, several objects were missing.

The wheels.

Set up on cinder blocks, the car looked like an aged brick. The steering wheel was gone, as were the seats and sections of the interior paneling. Wiring and steel framework were visible like bones on a carcass.

Reed's eyes flicked to Jackson's truck, a far newer and more expensive vehicle, but it was untouched. He'd waxed it recently and it glimmered in the light. Shocked at the robbery, he turned to Jackson, who bore a smirk on his face.

"Need a ride to class?" he asked, sliding on his sunglasses.

Reed blinked in recognition. "Kate?"

"Who else?" Jackson asked.

Reed began to laugh and approached his stripped car. As he drew close he spotted a note on the front seat. He unlocked the door and swung it open. Picking up the note, he unfolded it to reveal a message written from lettering cut from magazines.

Your car has proven inadequate. If you want to see your car whole again, be ready on June 21st at 6:00. It's time you drove a real car.

Jackson leaned over his shoulder. "She seems to have taken issue with your car breaking down."

"But what does she mean by a real car?" he asked.

"You'll find out on Thursday," he said with a smirk. "Right now, we should get to class."

"How did she do this?" Reed asked, sweeping a hand at the car.

"Marta's cousin is a mechanic," Jackson said.

"He did this?"

"Kate and her roommates came with him last night," Jackson said. "Apparently they wanted to have a part in dismantling your car."

"You saw it all?"

"I watched from the window," he admitted. "I was supposed to keep you inside but you went to bed early. It was surprising how fast they finished."

"When do I get it back?" Reed asked, finally turning away from his demolished car.

"I suppose when you agree to accept the date," Jackson said, unlocking the door.

As they pulled onto the road, Reed took out his phone to text Kate, but hesitated, an idea forming in his mind. It had never occurred to him before, but then, he'd never had a girl ask him on a date before—not like this.

A sly smile spread on his face as he mulled it over, considering the ramifications of responding to the invite in such a manner. Kate clearly thought she had him figured out, but if he did this, it would make for an incredible surprise.

"What's that smile for?" Jackson asked, accelerating onto the main road.

"If I needed your help to answer her invite, would you help?"

He cracked a smile. "Is it going to be fun?"

"Definitely."

"Then I'm in," Jackson said. "What's your plan?"

Reed detailed his idea of how he intended to answer Kate's invitation. It wasn't complicated, but the preparation would be a challenge. It would also show Kate what he felt, a fact not lost on Jackson.

"This is going to show Kate you like her," he said. "A lot. Are you sure you want to do that?"

"She went out on a limb to tell me what she felt," Reed said. "I need her to know that I feel the same."

"Without saying you're committed," Jackson finished.

"Exactly."

Jackson came to a stop at a light next to the stadium and leaned back in his seat. "We're going to need a freezer. A big one."

"You think Marta will help?" Reed asked. "Her uncle owns a restaurant, doesn't he?"

"Of course," Jackson said with a smirk. "Ember may be the ringleader, but Marta is just as clever."

"You'll have to drive me around," Reed said. "We'll have to move fast to set it up, but it will take time to freeze."

"She's going to wonder why she hasn't gotten a response."

"I'll take care of that," Reed said.

His phone was still in hand, so he sent a quick text to Kate. **Not feeling well this morning. Can I text you later?**

Evidently expecting a response after he'd seen his car, her answer was quick in coming. **Do you need medicine? Can you not make it to class?**

The first question was obviously intended to console, while the second was trying to see if he'd seen his car. He considered his response carefully and then typed back.

I think I'll be fine. I'll take something and go back to bed.

Do you want me to stop by after work?

It would be nice to see you, but I don't want you to get sick. I'll call you when I wake up.

Okay. Hope you feel better.

"What did you say?" Jackson asked.

"That I'm not feeling well," Reed said. "It's true enough. Walking out to see your car stripped to the bones is guaranteed to make you sick."

Jackson nodded and glanced at the clock on the dash. "You think we have time before your class?"

"I'll be late," he said. "But Dr. Caldin will understand."

"Are you sure about this?" Jackson asked.

"I just bought us some time," Reed said, smiling at the image of Kate's face. "Let's make it count . . ."

Chapter 2

They drove to the store and he jogged in, returning a moment later with a single rose, fishing line, and wood. Dropping the wood into the truck bed, he kept the rose and the fishing line and got back into the truck.

"I called Marta," Jackson said. "She already talked to her mom and she said we could use the freezer in the back."

Reed laughed to himself. "Marta's family just robbed me, and now they're helping me. Have you ever considered how bizarre this has become?"

"Love is like that," Jackson said. "It gets out of hand."

"And what would you know about love?" Reed asked.

Jackson grinned and pointed to the glove compartment. "See for yourself."

Reed opened the glove compartment and found a small box. His breathe caught as he pulled it out and flipped it open—to find a ring. He swiveled in his seat and raised it with a questioning look.

"Are you serious?" Reed asked.

"I've had it for a couple weeks," Jackson said, a broad smile on his face. "I just haven't figured out how to propose."

"I don't believe it," Reed said.

He suddenly became aware of the two women standing outside the truck. They'd been walking by on their way into the store and came to a halt, their expressions lit with amusement. Reed suddenly realized he was holding the ring up to Jackson, who was still smiling.

He snapped the ring box shut and waved at the women. They gave him a thumbs-up and walked away. Reed and Jackson exchanged a look and burst into a laugh. Then Jackson put the truck into reverse and backed out.

"I knew you loved her," Reed said. "I just didn't know you wanted to propose."

"I have you to blame," Jackson said. "When you started your thesis, I thought I'd humor you, but going on the dates you planned made me realize just how much I care about her. Then one day I decided I never wanted to play another game without her on my team. That's when I knew."

"Should I apologize or say thank you?" Reed asked.

"Both," Jackson said. "Because I want you to be the best man—if she says yes."

"She will," Reed said confidently.

Jackson grinned, but the expression bore a trace of nervousness. "I hope so. Will you help me plan the proposal?"

"Of course," Reed replied. "But you shouldn't keep this in the car. It's not very safe. After all, my car got stripped in the driveway."

Jackson laughed and agreed, and shortly after, they pulled into the restaurant that Marta's family owned. As they were unloading, Marta parked next to them and got out of the car. Clearly excited, she helped pick up the wood.

"Are you sure this is going to work?" Marta asked.

"Positive," Reed said.

They walked around back and approached the kitchen door. Marta's uncle opened the door and ushered them inside, waving to the freezer door at the back. It was still early but he'd already begun to cook, and savory smells filled the kitchen.

They carried their loads to an open corner and Reed directed them in the assembly. Using the tools from Jackson's truck, they screwed the boards onto the plywood and Reed sealed the gaps with caulk. When they were done the pieces had become a big wooden box.

"We should put it on a cart," Jackson said. "It's going to be heavy when it's done."

"Good idea," Reed said, and then looked to Marta at the stove. "How's the boiling water coming?"

"Almost ready," she called. She had nearly every pot on the stove.

Marta's uncle appeared and shook his head. "Why boil water you intend to freeze?" he asked.

"It's the only way for the ice to come out clear," Reed said.

Cutting the fishing line, he tied it to the corners of the box and hung the rose in the center. Servers and Marta's family visited often to observe, and on occasion, help. They laughed and talked about his intentions like they were part of the event.

When the water was finished they poured it into the box. Reed was careful to check the seals to make sure none leaked out. Servers jumped in to help lug the pots of boiling water to the box, laughing as they added it to the box.

"It's going to be a three-foot ice cube," Jackson said, wiping sweat from his brow.

"With a rose inside," Reed said.

After the last bucket had been poured they gently pushed the makeshift ice tray into the freezer and set back to examine their handiwork. Jackson grinned, imagining Kate's face when she found it on her porch.

"Let's go," Reed said, and then looked at the clock on the wall. "But I think I missed class."

"Priorities," Jackson said. "I'll drop you off and you can explain it to your professor."

"I'll let you know when it's frozen," Maria said, and then abruptly pulled Reed into a hug. "And take care of that girl."

"I will," Reed said, surprised and gratified by the gesture.

They gathered their things and cleaned up the workspace before heading out. Jackson smirked as several of the other waitresses whispered about how romantic the gesture would be. They stepped outside and got back into the truck before heading back to campus.

"Kate might stop by," Jackson said.

"I'll hang out at home after I talk to Dr. Caldin," Reed said. "Just in case."

"Just how long will it take to freeze?" Jackson asked.

"It's in a freezer that's colder than a normal freezer," Reed said. "I hope it doesn't take too long, but it might."

"You can't fake sick for long," Jackson warned. "She's smart. She'll get suspicious."

"True," he said. "But I think I have till tomorrow morning to discover my car. Finding it will give us more time before she'll expect an answer."

"Then we just let the freezer do its work," Jackson said.

They stopped at the campus and Jackson said he'd pick Reed up after his own class. Reed made his way to class and spoke to Dr. Caldin, who let him take the quiz he'd missed. When he finished, he gave his teacher the paper.

"Thanks for letting me take the quiz," he said.

Dr. Caldin peered over his glasses. "Least I could do. Good luck with your research."

Reed grinned and left. As he walked to where Jackson would pick him up, he pulled out his phone and messaged Kate. Throughout the day he did his best to keep her from realizing he was stalling. But as Jackson had said, her texts began to sound suspicious, with Jackson confirming she'd reached out to him in an attempt to get an answer.

The next morning he sent her a message.

So…you wouldn't know anything about me being robbed, would you?

Nope, came the reply. **Unless you agree to the date.**

You know I'm going to say yes.

I hoped.

You'll have your answer by tonight, he replied, and then added a smiley face.

The silence indicated she didn't know how to respond to that, and he grinned at the image of her confusion. Several times the dots appeared as she tried to write back but didn't. Finally she said,

I look forward to it.

He showed Jackson the text string when he arrived later that day and Jackson grunted in amusement. "She doesn't know what's happening."

"That's how we surprise her," Reed said. "Let's go get the block of ice."

They piled into his truck and drove to the restaurant, arriving just as it was closing. Several of Marta's cousins had stayed late to help them load the enormous ice cube, and they even offered to follow Reed to help unload it at Kate's house.

"Which one of you stripped my car?" Reed asked.

They all looked to one and he grinned sheepishly. "I'm Roman."

"You can help," Reed said.

Eager to do so, he jumped into the truck and they drove to Kate's house. Jackson sent a message to Marta to confirm they would not be seen and then eased the truck into the driveway. With great care they carried the cube to the porch. Reed winced as he undid the strap, the sound emitting a soft *ting* as it came apart. Jackson shoved a screwdriver between the wood and the board and it came loose. Moments later they had the wood off and they retreated to the truck. Jackson moved the truck up the street and then they returned to the bushes.

"Be right back," Reed said.

He darted to the door and rang the doorbell, and then sprinted to the bushes. His heart hammering in his chest, he dove into the shadows just as the door opened and Kate appeared.

Chapter 3

Kate stared at the giant ice cube, her features twisted into a cute expression of confusion. Then she noticed the note he'd placed on the top and reached out for it. She unfolded it and Reed recalled the words as she read them.

To be your date,

would melt my heart,

To drive at your side,

While my car's apart.

You must find the rose,

So the race may start.

"Your rhyme was stupid," Jackson said.

"It's romantic," Roman said.

"What do you know?"

"I'm Latin." Roman smirked. "Romance is in my blood."

"How old are you?" Jackson asked.

"Seventeen," he replied defensively.

"Can you two be quiet?" Reed asked.

Kate's roommates were all standing on the porch. They exulted over the note and the giant ice cube, with Marta giving a command performance of feigned shock. In the midst of speculation and awe, Kate stared at the rose, perfectly frozen in clear ice, a soft smile on her face.

Reed watched her, a tingle climbing up his spine as he witnessed her response. He'd seen that expression on countless dates, but this time was different. Kate's smile conveyed so much more than surprise and wonder, it conveyed a tenderness, a vulnerability, an intimacy.

She didn't know he was watching, but he felt like she was looking right at him, like he was on the porch inches from touching her hand. She flushed at something Brittney said and brushed her hand across the enormous ice cube.

"Looks like it's a hit," Jackson murmured.

The girls pulled out hair dryers to try and melt the ice. Ember said that was cheating and took pictures while Brittney wielded two hair dryers, gunslinger style. The others laughed but their combined efforts didn't make a dent on the cube.

"It's going to take forever," Ember complained.

"That's our cue," Jackson said. "Let's go."

Reluctant to depart, Reed watched Kate until Jackson tugged on his arm. Then he turned and crept through the shadows. When they were clear he stood and walked back to the truck, and the whole way Reed bore a smile on his face.

"That's a confident smile," Jackson said.

"Oh?" he asked.

Jackson stabbed a finger at him. "You've made your decision, haven't you."

"Maybe," Reed said, but his smile widened.

Seeing Kate had caused something to click. For the first time since the start of the dating challenge, he felt like he knew what he wanted. And he wanted Kate. More than anything he'd ever wanted in his life, he wanted to be with her.

His promise to Aura remained unfulfilled, and he would always regret it, but if he abandoned Kate now he would never forgive himself. He yearned to be with her, every moment of every day, and now that he could see without the filter of regret, he realized she'd become essential to every aspect of his life.

"About time," Jackson said, unlocking the door.

"For what?" Roman asked, looking between them as if he'd missed part of the conversation.

They piled into the truck and Reed jerked his head. "I didn't say anything," he said, his tone gaining an edge. "And don't say anything to her roommates."

Jackson raised his hands. "What's there to say?"

Reed smiled. "If there is something to say, I want to say it at the right time."

"My lips are sealed," Jackson replied, turning up the street and leaving Kate's house behind. "But are you going to say it tonight?"

Reed shook his head. "She has her date planned, and I've intruded enough. Besides, after all our dates, I think she deserves a grand finale, don't you think?"

"Is this about your car?" Roman asked.

Reed and Jackson laughed in unison. "It's not about the car," Reed said. "But I really need it later this week. Jackson can't be my chauffeur every day."

"True," Jackson said.

"Well if you ever decide to sell your car, I'm buying," he said.

"You want his wreck?" Jackson asked.

"For cheap," Roman said.

Just then Reed's phone buzzed and he saw it was Kate. Warning his companions to silence, he answered the call and, at Jackson's insistence, put it on speaker.

"Hello?"

"Don't 'hello' me," she said. "There's a giant ice cube on my porch with a rose frozen inside."

Reed heard the smile in her voice, just audible over the sound of hair dryers. "I take it you accept my answer?"

She laughed lightly. "Of course—assuming I can get to it. The rose was a nice touch, by the way."

"I couldn't leave you just a giant box of ice," Reed said. "That would just be weird."

She laughed again. "It's going to take forever to melt the thing."

"No it's not!" Ember called in the background. "I've summoned reinforcements."

"You could just pour hot water on it," Reed said.

The sound quieted as Kate changed rooms. Then her voice became softer, more mischievous. "I know, but I'm waiting for them to figure it out. They're really enjoying melting it with hair dryers."

Jackson grinned and whispered, "She's positively devious."

"Call me when you finish the melting," Reed said.

"I will," she replied. "And your car will be back to normal by tomorrow. I'll call the one who helped take it apart."

"Roman?" Reed asked, glancing at Marta's cousin. "He's a good kid."

"Hey!" Roman said.

"He's with you?" Kate asked in surprise.

"I needed help with the delivery and someone had a guilty conscience."

"I did not," Roman protested. "I just wanted to see her face."

"You were outside?" Kate asked.

"Maybe," Reed admitted.

The sound of laughter and giggling rose a notch as more voices joined the party, and Kate called out to them. The flurry of giggles implied girls were arriving by the minute. Then she shifted position again and lowered her voice once more.

"I'm being summoned for a picture. Call you tonight?"

"Of course," he said. "And how about lunch tomorrow? Not a date, just hanging out."

Her voice indicated she was surprised, and a little suspicious. "More meddling in my date?"

"No," he said. "I promise. I'd just like to go to lunch. But you'll have to pick me up, as I don't think my car will be un-robbed in time."

She laughed. "Deal. I'll pick you up at one."

They said their goodbyes and hung up, whereupon Jackson nudged him. "Looks like I'm not the only one that's fallen hard."

"Are you going to be able to keep this to yourself?" Reed asked.

"I won't say anything," he said, but when Reed skewered him with a look he raised a hand. "I promise I won't tell anyone."

"Even Shelby?"

He sighed. "Even Shelby."

Reed turned on Roman but he raised his hands in protest. "I was just here to deliver the ice," he said, a smile tugging at the corners of his lips. "I promise not to say anything about what I don't understand with anyone who might have an interest in said non-knowledge."

Reed and Jackson both looked at him and he shrugged. "I won't say anything."

Jackson turned onto the street that would take them back to the restaurant. "Do you know what you're going to do in two weeks?"

"I do—but I'm not telling you," Reed said. "Not this time. I'm keeping it to myself. I'm not going to risk Kate finding anything out."

"But you know what you're going to do?"

"It's going to be on the Fourth of July," Reed said. "That's all I'll say."

Jackson pressed him on it, but Reed refused to budge. After all the going back and forth, Reed couldn't risk anything he said getting back to Kate. Or her roommates. If he was going to cross that bridge with her, she would be the first to know.

"Good luck with everything," Roman said as he got out. Then he grinned. "I may have to steal your techniques to use on my girl."

"Feel free," Reed said.

He grinned and shut the door, and as they drove home Reed continued to resist Jackson's efforts for a glimpse into his plans. It would be difficult enough to keep his decision to himself—especially from Kate. The burning in his heart yearned to be shared, but after all the creative dates it felt wrong to just call her up and tell her. He needed to plan something special.

"Just make sure you don't downplay it too much on your date this week," Jackson warned as they parked back at their house. "A surprise is great, but if she thinks you're being too cold, she might get the wrong idea."

"Good point," Reed said. "But what about . . .?" he gestured to the glove compartment, where the engagement ring was sloppily hidden.

"Oh," Jackson said, reaching out and retrieving the ring box. He stuffed it into his pocket. "You keep my secret, I'll keep yours. We can plan something after you seal the deal with Kate."

Reed frowned. "And by seal the deal you mean . . ."

Jackson rolled his eyes. "I mean kiss her. I know you're not going to have sex with the girl. Honestly, it's like you were born in the wrong century."

91

Reed laughed. "Stop smiling so much, or Shelby's going to know something's up."

"I'll try," Jackson said as they walked inside.

He failed.

Chapter 4

Shelby pounced the moment they walked inside. "What's going on?" she asked.

They exchanged a grin and spoke in unison. "Nothing."

"I just spoke to Brittney," she said. "Something going on and I want to know what."

She folded her arms and pursed her lips, so Reed stepped forward. "You'll know soon enough. For now, can you trust me?"

Shelby grunted in irritation, but after a moment she relaxed and returned her attention to Jackson. "A girl doesn't like to be kept in the dark."

Taking the opportunity to escape, Reed slipped into his room and picked up a pad and pen. Then he set to planning his date for the Fourth of July. The holiday provided unique opportunities, and he scrapped several before he settled on one he liked. He sat back in his seat and mulled it over, a smile forming on his face.

The rest of the week he squeezed in as much time as possible with Kate. He knew it might be playing his hand—and Kate's measuring looks indicated she was suspicious—but he couldn't resist. Aside from a lingering twinge about Aura, he was ready to take things forward with Kate.

The prospect both excited and terrified him. As much as he'd dated, he'd never dated anyone for real, so it would be uncharted waters. Still, he figured Kate would be the perfect instructor. The challenge would be to not give anything away, until he was ready.

The night of Kate's date came and he was ready. His car had been fully restored to its former lack of glory, and they passed it on the way to her car. Kate patted it affectionately as they passed, as if it were an aged dog.

"Where did you store all the pieces?" Reed asked as he climbed into her car.

"Roman stored them at his work, a small mechanic shop on the north slope."

"I still can't believe you stripped my car," Reed said, his tone one of admiration. "The neighbors were coming over every day questioning what had happened. I even had a cop stop by."

He marveled at how comfortable their conversation was. It would be so easy to just reach out and touch her hand, to feel the softness of her skin. He wondered how she would react if he just leaned over and kissed her on the cheek. He swallowed as heat flooded his skin and looked out the window.

"Is our whole date tonight intended to make fun of my car breaking down?" he asked. "Or just the invite?"

"The whole date," she admitted with a smile. "How are you at driving go-karts?"

"Really?" he asked. "It's not enough that you dismantle my car? Now you want to humiliate me on the racetrack?"

"Yes," she said.

He laughed. "How do you know I'm not great?"

"Because your car does zero to sixty in the time the earth revolves around the sun."

"Hey," he protested. "It does better than that—marginally better, but better."

"We'll see your driving skills soon enough," she said smugly.

"I take it you've done this before?" he asked.

"A little," she said.

"How many times is a little?" he asked suspiciously.

"A lot."

"I may surprise you," he said.

"I hope so," she said.

Their eyes met and she smiled. He smiled in turn and looked away. It would be so easy to tell her in that moment, but after planning his date, he knew the moment he wanted to tell her what he felt and finally pull her into a kiss . . .

"Just wait and see," he said softly.

Her smile widened and she pulled onto the freeway, heading east towards the edge of town. Their conversation shifted to the melting of the ice cube, which took much longer than it should have, even with nine girls armed with hair dryers. Unfortunately, it was not quite frozen in the center. The ice became thin and suddenly broke, splashing freezing water on several of the girls, leading a round of laughter. When Kate was finally able to lift the rose from the ice, the girls had cheered.

"I think they're all in love with you," she said. "I can't tell you how many asked about your schedule."

"It's rather full," he replied.

Her eyebrows pulled together in confusion, but he did not clarify. She hesitated, but whatever she was about to say she kept to herself. A moment later they pulled into the parking lot of the go-kart racetrack.

When they got out Reed had to resist the urge to reach out to her, as if it was the most natural thing in the world. She smiled shyly, her hands twitching as if she too felt it, and she put her hands in her pockets. But like two magnets struggling to be one, they walked close to each other, allowing their shoulders to touch with every step.

They walked in and Reed was surprised to find it empty. He'd expected a crowd, but the only one present was a young man at the counter. Dressed in greasy overalls and a grungy t-shirt, he was hunched over the desk. He looked up at their entry.

"Roman?" Reed asked in surprise.

"Hey, Reed," he said with a smile. "Glad you could make it."

"What are you doing here?" he asked.

Roman gestured to the place. "I work here. I said I was a mechanic—I didn't say of cars."

"And you let him demolish my car?" Reed asked.

"I didn't always do small engines," he said.

Kate gestured to Roman. "Marta said her cousin knew about cars. When I talked to him about the track he suggested we kidnap your car."

"You didn't have to tell him that," Roman said in an aside.

"I can't be mad," Reed said, "you already wiped the slate clean."

Roman grinned and walked around the counter. He opened the back door, leading them onto the track, which proved to be a complex figure that turned in and back on itself, even going over a bridge and curving back to go under. Lit by large halogen lights, the track glowed.

"Our grand reopening is this weekend," Roman said. "I'm supposed to be testing all the karts and I asked if I could have a few friends help. The owner was kind enough to say yes."

"So we have the track to ourselves?" Reed asked.

"Just you two," he replied, picking up two clipboards with release forms. "Sorry, but everyone has to sign. You ever done this before?"

Reed nodded and took the paper, signing as Roman reviewed the rules. Three laps on the track, no contact between the carts (but a little was okay), and watch the warning lights. He added to be careful on the turns and take them slow if they were uncertain. Then he picked up two helmets, using one to point at the two gleaming carts at the starting line.

"These are the best I have. I prefer the blue one, but red is just as fast."

"He can have blue," Kate said, taking a helmet. "He'll need the advantage."

Reed laughed as he donned his own helmet and tightened the strap. Then he climbed into the blue kart and buckled up. He felt a familiar thrill as he settled into the seat and called out to Roman as he was walking away.

"Alcohol and gas mixture? Or any nitrous?"

Roman raised an eyebrow, as did Kate, who swiveled in her seat to stare at him.

"Alcohol and gas," Roman said. "Looks like you do know a thing or two."

Reed grinned and turned the key to start his kart. Then he nodded his readiness. Kate did the same and they pumped the gas, revving the engines. Her pealing laughter echoed over the sound of the engines and both looked to the lights positioned above the track.

"Racers ready?" Roman's voice came over a speaker.

Reed nodded, and in his peripheral vision he watched Kate do the same. A signal pinged and the red light changed to orange, the lights moving down towards the green. Reed tightened his grip on the steering wheel and released the parking brake. The anticipation mounted as the lights continued to ping, three seconds, then two. He glanced at Kate and saw her looking at him, her eyes bright with amusement and excitement. Then he looked to the lights and they turned green, and both karts leapt across the starting line.

Chapter 5

They raced up the first stretch and into a turn, putting Kate on the inside as she steered into the curve. Reed hung with her, accelerating around the outside and into a short straightaway. Then the track banked left. As Kate slowed for the turn Reed punched it, pulling on the brake as he drifted around the corner, his tires squealing.

He grinned as he swerved past her and into the lead, the tight turn pushing him several feet ahead of Kate's kart. Over the squeal of tires and growling engines he heard Kate shout, but he was already gone. Accelerating into another drift, he swerved around the corner and sped away, leaving Kate in the dust.

Speeding around the corners, he relished the pull of the kart, the familiar feel of the tires slipping on the concrete. Three times around the track and he came to a screeching halt across the finish line. He turned off the engine and a moment later she stopped beside him. Then she yanked her helmet off and glared.

"What in the—"

The door clattered open and Roman appeared in the opening. "You just beat the lap record—*my* lap record. How did you do that?"

Reed pulled off his helmet and stepped out of the kart. "After my parents split up my dad decided he wanted to start a small business, and bought a go-kart track in a neighboring town. Part of the agreement was for the previous owner to show my dad how to run the place. The guy used to be a professional racer so he *really* knew how to drive. I spent most of the first month racing with him. Within a year my dad had driven the track into the ground, but I still remember how to drive."

Kate began to laugh, the sound building with amusement and chagrin. "Did you know this was our date for the night?" She glanced at Roman as if he'd betrayed her, but he raised his hands helplessly.

"No idea," Reed said. "But the moment you said go-karts all the memories came flooding back."

"Get back in your kart," she said. "You're going to teach me how to do that."

Reed raised an eyebrow and looked to Roman. "We might clip the walls a bit."

"I have time to fix it," Roman said, and then smiled. "I'll watch you and then practice it on my own. I can already imagine Jerry's face when I show him what I can do."

He disappeared and Reed sank back into the kart. Then Kate called out to him. "You know, I wasn't prepared for this."

"For the track?" Reed asked, pausing in donning his helmet.

"For all the surprises," she said, her eyes on him. "I keep thinking I have you figured out, but then you come up with something like this." She swept her hand at the track.

"I haven't driven a kart in fifteen years," he said. "Not since my dad lost the track. It's not exactly a normal topic of conversation."

"You never took a date to do it?"

Reed cocked his head to the side. "Actually, no. After my dad's business tanked he was depressed for a while, so I made a point not to bring it up. I guess the habit carried into adulthood."

"Any other secret talents I should know about?" she asked.

He grinned. "They're best discovered on their own."

She matched his smile. "So how do we do this?"

While still parked, he described how to pull the brake right as you turned the steering wheel, how to backspin the wheel so the tires kept the kart from spinning out, and when to release the brake and press on the gas, accelerating out of the turn into a straightaway.

"Try to stay in the center of the turn for now," he said. "When you know how the kart is going to react, then you can bring it closer to the inside wall."

"But you didn't know that kart," she said shrewdly.

"True," he said. "So maybe I was trying to get your attention a little bit."

"Only a little?"

"Did it work?"

She grinned. "I like it fast." Then she flushed and shoved her helmet on. "Ready when you are."

"I'll go first," he said. "Stay behind me and only pull a little on the brake. Then we'll take it faster."

He gunned the engine and accelerated but kept well below top speed. Coming up on the first curve he did as he'd explained—moderate speed and moderate pull on the brake. Then he slowed on the opposite side and looked back. Kate turned into the curve at the right angle and braked, but didn't turn into the skid. The kart spun out and bounced lightly off the wall.

"Sorry Roman!" she shouted.

His voice came over the intercom. "Like I said, I can fix it."

"I can testify to that!" Reed called.

Kate laughed and turned her cart forward once more. When she waved her readiness, Reed did the same, leading her into the long curve. He'd forgotten to say she would need more speed with the longer curve, and she came to a stop halfway through.

For the next hour he taught her how to skid around the corners, coaching her until she could pull off a respectable drift. Roman requested a turn, and Reed and Kate sat in the small bleachers overlooking the track.

Reed was conscious of their proximity but did not move away. After doing the track several times, it felt good to sit in the open and stretch, and he enjoyed watching Roman attempt the skid.

"Please tell me I did better than that," Kate said, gesturing to Roman spinning on the track.

Reed sipped on the Sprite they had gotten from the concession stand. "You did."

"Really?" she asked.

"Really," he said. "He's doing well, but he has too many habits. You had less experience so you could learn easier."

She smiled as Roman hit the guardrail again. His curse was audible from their seats in the bleachers. He backed up and tried again. Night had fallen and so had the temperature. Kate scooted closer to Reed.

"It's funny how everyone has random things from their past," Kate said. "Did you know Brittney is a really good artist?"

"Seriously?"

"She got into it as a kid," Kate said. "I didn't know until I saw her collection of pencils on her desk and asked."

"Everyone has a past," Reed said. "It would take a lifetime to truly know another person."

"So tell me something else about yourself," she said, opening a bag of chips.

Reed considered her request. "I got stitches on my forehead when I was two. My sister and I were playing king of the mountain and she pushed me off. I hit a cabinet and split my head open." He held up his hair to show the scar, a thin line just above his ear.

"I got this two years ago," she said, lifting her sleeve to show a wide scar on her shoulder. "Bake and Tyler were practicing knife fighting in the kitchen and it grew heated. I was foolish enough to intervene and caught a knife in the shoulder."

He reached out and traced a line down the scar. Knobby and wide, it had obviously been a small but ugly wound. Her eyes widened at his touch and he realized the intimacy of the contact, of his hand caressing her shoulder. Their eyes met and he withdrew his fingers.

"I thought you said no physical contact."

"Let's just say the lines are becoming blurry."

She raised an eyebrow and studied his expression, but he smiled and looked away. She opened her mouth to speak and then shut it. Before she could decide what to say, Roman managed to drift around a corner, his ensuing shout of victory echoing off the track walls.

"He's getting better," she said.

"Habits aren't so hard to change," he said.

"Really?" she asked, incredulous. "I've been trying to break the habit of hitting snooze on the alarm clock for years."

"On which days *do* you wake up on time?" he asked.

"When I have a reason that forces me from the warm comfort of my incredibly soft blankets."

"Exactly," he said. "Breaking a habit is easy."

She frowned. "I don't understand what you mean. How is this easy?"

"You're just missing the key ingredient," he said, and met her gaze. "Any habit can be broken . . . if you have the right motivation."

Her eyebrows knit together as she studied his expression. He didn't want to tell her that he'd made his choice, but he did want to make his stance clear. She began to smile, the expression spreading to lighten her features.

"Care for another race?" she asked, gesturing to the track.

"Always," he said, his eyes on her.

Chapter 6

They continued to race until it got late, and by then Kate had improved significantly—an irritation to Roman, who had yet to do as well. Bidding him farewell, they walked out to her car and climbed in.

"We stayed later than I thought," Kate said, eyeing the clock on the dash.

"It's past eleven," Reed said, surprised at how quickly the time had flown.

"I was going to take you to an ice cream place a few miles from here. They serve a dish called the race track, which has a car made of candy on top of a chocolate and vanilla waffle cone."

"You think they're still open?" he asked, loathe to end the date.

"We'll get back after midnight," she said. "Unless that's another rule you're willing to bend on."

"Let's go," he said. "But not too late."

She pulled onto the road. "Next thing I know, you're going to want sex in the back seat."

He grinned and shook his head. "I don't drive that fast."

She laughed and turned onto the main road, accelerating toward the highway. As they drove away Reed found himself wishing he was still racing with Kate. In an odd way they'd been close. Separated by car and space, they had nevertheless woven around each other, the cars occasionally touching.

"I still can't believe you drive a go-kart like that," she said.

He smiled. "I played a lot of Mario kart at the time, and it felt like the real thing. Mario kart lost its appeal afterward."

"I bet it did," she said. "Nothing like the real thing."

"True," he said.

"Did you ever beat him?" she asked. "The professional racer?"

"A few times," he said. "But I'm pretty sure he let me win."

"That's nice of him."

"Those were the times he was sober," he said. "It was tough to tell, though. He and my dad drank a lot."

She got off at the next exit and followed the directions on her phone to the ice cream shop. They pulled in and the sign revealed it was about to close, so they rushed in to place their order. With Race Track Supremes in hand, they settled into her car and ate as the entire strip mall went dark.

"This is surprisingly good," he said.

"Roman mentioned it," she replied. "I figured it went with the theme."

"Are you getting tired of planning these dates yet?" he asked.

She swiveled in her seat to look at him. "Are you?"

"It's different, planning for one person over several dates. I'm used to just one or two, or occasionally three dates with the same girl. This is our tenth, and even though I've only planned half of them, it's proving to be an increasing challenge."

"You didn't answer the question," she said.

"Neither did you," he countered.

She tipped her spoon as if to say, *fair point*. Her gaze lingered on him, gauging the purpose of his conversation, and he tried to keep his expression mildly curious. He was curious, but if they were going to elevate their relationship, he wanted to see what she wanted. But was he saying too much? Eventually she shrugged.

"When I was a little girl I watched movies and read books that always talked about adventure. I remember wondering what an adventure would be like, and fell asleep many times imagining my own. I never thought I'd get one."

"You really feel that way?"

"I do," she said. "There may not be dragons or knights, but this adventure certainly has magic." She smiled coyly, making him laugh. "Now your turn. Are you tired of it yet?"

"When we started this game, I thought I would crush you," he admitted. "I never thought you would prove such a formidable adversary."

"I hope that's not all you see," she said.

"Poor word choice," he said. "I just mean you've surprised me—and continue to do so. I never thought this game would become an obsession."

"Now I'm an obsession?" Her lips twitched with amusement.

He grunted ruefully. "I seem to have a talent for finding the wrong words tonight."

"I won't hold that against you," she said. "Especially since you're still in the lead."

"What do you mean?" he asked.

"My roommates keep a tally," she admitted. "And you're still in the lead—not by much, mind you, but enough. The island date gave you a big advantage."

"The one where we fell in the pool?" he asked, incredulous.

"They call it the one where I took a shower in your house," she said. "Ember thought it was the closest you and I came to spending the night."

"True or not," he said, "I'm glad to know I have the lead."

"Don't sound so smug," she said, throwing a napkin at him. "Tomorrow they'll post the picture of us at the track, and the details of the night. You can see for yourself if you'd like. Ember put it online after I used the band in the library. It's getting a following and people are voting."

Reed pulled out his phone and followed her direction to the site, surprised to find an image of himself standing with Kate. The picture had been taken of them on their third date, and the way they looked at each other implied exactly what they felt.

"I can't believe she posted it online," he said.

"Does that bother you?" she asked. "There are thousands of people posting now. There's even a Creative Dating hashtag about us."

"I had no idea."

"Are you upset?"

He considered her question but then shook his head. "I always wanted my methods of dating to become more commonplace. By the tone of these comments, it seems to be having an impact. Turns out all I needed was you."

"Truest statement you've ever made," she said fervently, and they both laughed.

They finished their ice cream and stepped out to drop the napkins and spoons into a trash can. Then she drove him home. On the way he read some of the comments aloud, surprised and gratified by the praise some of the girls seemed to be heaping upon them.

"They're calling you the new age woman," he said.

"Hardly," Kate said, pulling into his driveway.

They got out and she walked him to his door, but Reed found himself looking around, wondering if someone was taking a picture of them. They reached his porch and he embraced her, and once again she lingered in his arms. For the first time, he did not feel the sting of regret, and smiled as he held her to his chest. When they parted she had a knowing smile on her face.

"I'll expect your invite," she said.

"Be ready," he said with a smile. "I have to maintain my lead."

She laughed and walked to her car, glancing back as she got in. "I look forward to what's coming."

He could not restrain his smile. "You should," he said.

Volume 11: The Fireworks Date

Chapter 1

"What is Reed waiting for?" Marta asked. "He should have asked you out for your next date by now."

"I don't know," Kate said.

Kate looked down and realized she'd been fidgeting with her napkin so much that it had torn. With an effort she put it back on the table and leaned back in the bench, causing the vinyl to creak.

"Your date is tomorrow," Ember said, demolishing a roll. "What's taking him so long?"

Kate and the blondes were sitting at dinner at Marta's restaurant. It was the third of July, just one day before they were supposed to go on a date, but Reed had yet to extend an invitation. She reflexively pulled out her phone and looked at it, but there hadn't been an answer since they'd talked earlier that day.

Brittney frowned. "Have you asked him what he's waiting for?"

"She can't do that," Ember protested. "It will show how nervous she is."

"I'm not nervous," Kate said.

"Liar," Marta said, pointing at Kate's fork.

Kate looked down and realized she was now tapping her fork against her knife. She grimaced and put the fork down, annoyed that her hands continued to betray her nervousness. Then she leaned forward and lowered her voice.

"We talk every day, now," she said. "And I see him almost as often."

Despite her concern, Kate smiled. Over the last two weeks they'd been together almost constantly. They weren't dates, at least not in the context of the challenge, but they went out for lunch or breakfast whenever the opportunity allowed. Sometimes they just sat together watching a movie with Jackson and Shelby or the blondes.

But the tension was past the breaking point, and every time they were together she wanted to grab his neck and yank him into a kiss. She swallowed and forced the image from her mind, sipping her water in an effort to cool the heat in her belly.

"You saw him yesterday," she said. "When he came over for Brittney's dinner night."

"He hasn't mentioned your date at all?" Brittney asked.

Kate shook her head. "He hasn't said a word about tomorrow night."

"He didn't forget," Brittney said. "Did he?" She glanced at Ember.

Ember folded her arms, her expression like a grizzled detective. "No. He's up to something."

Kate frowned, her eyebrows pulling together as she glared at her roommates with suspicious eyes. "Are *you* hiding something? You *did* invite me to dinner."

Brittney shook her head. "I don't know anything."

Ember scowled. "I wish I could say I knew, but I haven't heard anything."

They all looked to Marta, who shrugged. "I don't know anything, either. And I didn't invite you to dinner. My mom said we should come and eat . . ."

They all stared at her, the truth settling in. In that moment Marta's mother bustled up to the table and placed four rolls of silverware on the table. Then she pulled out a pad and paper and looked to them.

"You ready to order, girls . . .?" Her voice faded when all eyes settled on her

110

"Mother?" Marta asked. "Did Reed enlist you to get us here?"

"Of course not, dear." She waved her hand dismissively. "I'll come back when you know what you want."

"*Mother.*"

She tried to protest but Marta stood, trapping her mother between the tables. The woman's eyes flicked between Marta, Ember, and Brittney, and then settled on Kate, who raised an eyebrow. She grunted and waved her pen at them like a sword.

"I only know that he wanted you here tonight," she said.

"That's *all* you know?" Ember demanded.

Kate hid a smile. Seeing the indomitable Ember lock eyes with the indomitable mother was amusing, and she wondered who would blink first. But it was Marta's mother that scowled and jerked her head.

"He said he needed an hour to set up," she replied.

"That's why you took so long to get our bread," Marta accused.

"You're not going to leave, are you?" Maria asked anxiously. "He insisted I keep you here."

"We're going to leave," Ember said, rising to her feet.

"No," Kate said. "We're not." She smiled as they looked to her. "He wanted an hour? We'll give him an hour. But not a minute more."

"You don't want to go spy on him?" Ember asked.

Kate jerked her head. "I want to see the invitation when it's ready. If he waited this long, it had better be good. Let's not spoil it, shall we?"

Marta nodded reluctantly and took a seat. Brittney seemed relieved. Ember grunted in irritation and sank onto the bench. Shaking her head, Kate picked up the menu and rattled off her order. Marta's mother, clearly pleased, wrote their requests down and then departed. The moment she was gone Kate pulled out her phone.

"What are you doing?" Brittney asked.

"I said we're not going to see him," Kate said, a sly smile spreading on her features. "Doesn't mean I can't have a little fun."

They laughed and leaned in, helping her craft the first message.

Any chance you can talk? I'm out with my roommates and they won't stop talking about another guy they want to set me up with. I think I might go out with him tomorrow night. I mean, I don't have any plans yet...

The response was slow in coming, and they speculated as to the cause until their food came. Kate left her phone on the table so all could see when he replied. Just as they began to eat, the phone buzzed and she picked it up.

Oh? Is he cute?

Marta giggled. "He's on the lacrosse team."

"And studying to be a doctor," Brittney said. "We all love doctors." Then her smiled faded. "I'm sorry, Kate, I forgot that's what Jason is studying . . ."

Kate grinned and shook her head. "Jason is long gone," she said, marveling that she meant it. When Brittney had said *doctor* she hadn't even thought of Jason. It felt good to be truly over him.

"And say his dad is rich," Ember said.

"Why?" Kate asked, pausing in typing.

"Because we all want to date a guy with money," Ember reasoned. "We may not admit it, but money is attractive."

Kate shrugged and did as requested, filling in the details for the mythical date. Then she took a bite of bread and waited. This time the response came much faster, but Ember snatched her phone off the table. She read it and scowled.

"What?" Kate asked, taking it back.

Maria caved. Didn't she.

Ember swore under her breath. "How did he realize it so fast?"

112

"We tried to make him think Kate would go out with another guy," Brittney said. "We pushed it too far."

Ember swore again, but Marta laughed. "At least we know he's asking Kate tonight. Now we can relax and wait."

Kate grinned, her heart fluttering with anticipation. Reed was at her house, most likely setting up an invitation to ask her on a date. She'd wondered almost continuously since their last date if he would push their relationship to the next level, and the waiting had left her nervous and excited, the emotions rising to a fever pitch.

"Let's sneak out," she said.

"Really?" Ember asked.

Kate nodded. "I don't want to wait anymore. I want to see what he's up to."

"Kate," Brittney protested. "I'm hungry."

"You can eat after," Marta said, eyeing her mother. "We're going to have to run. I wouldn't put it past her to bar the door."

"Tell us when your mother isn't looking," Kate said.

She grinned, her heart rate accelerating as she leaned towards Brittney, trying to keep her readiness subtle. Then Marta nodded and they piled out of the booth. They threaded through the tables and sprinted to the door, escaping just as Marta's mother rotated and called out to them.

"Sorry," Marta cast over her shoulder.

They tumbled through the door into the parking lot but came to a collective halt. On the lawn in front of the restaurant a large sign had been erected. Hastily dug into the ground, the posts supported a large sheet of plywood. Fireworks had been fastened to the plywood in a strange pattern, and reflected an odd assortment of spinners, screamers, and sparklers. Mortars were mounted on the top, the fuses threaded down to connect with the other fuses. Then Kate realized all the fuses were threaded together, weaving into a single point sticking out the bottom corner. The door opened behind them and they turned to find Marta's mother, her expression smug.

"You *did* know more," Marta accused.

"Half of parenting is manipulation," she said with a smile.

"Did you even need an hour?"

"He said he needed ten minutes," she replied. "I promised twenty."

Kate pulled out her phone and realized they'd been inside the restaurant for exactly twenty-one minutes, long enough to sink the posts and mount the board of fireworks. As usual, Reed had planned every detail.

"Are you going to light it?" Marta's mother asked.

"I don't have a . . ."

Maria offered a lighter and Kate accepted it with a grateful nod. As Kate walked to the board, her roommates whipped out their phones and began to film. She stepped to the large arrow that pointed to the fuse, the lettering above indicating it needed to be lit. The sun had almost set and the night was dark, the timing obviously intentional.

She flicked the lighter and ignited the fuse, the fire licking upward and igniting a sparkler. It then caught and sparked its way onto the board, where it lit four sparklers, then six, and then she lost count. She retreated to her friends and held her breath.

Chapter 2

A spinner ignited and spun in a swirl of green sparks. Then the fuse lit a red one, followed by a yellow spinner. With nails through their center, they buzzed, sending sparks raining down on other fireworks igniting below.

Firecrackers went off like gunfire, crackling and exploding. A mortar detonated, sending a ball into the sky that erupted into a sphere of blue. Then a tank went off, firing screaming lights from the end of a wire.

A box of fireworks set on a shelf went off, showering the sign in sparks and light. Another mortar went off and then they all ignited in quick succession, filling the sky with bursts of light. More light erupted, the fireworks detonating in a sequence that flooded the lawn and street in light.

Cars slowed and drivers gawked from their windows, one narrowly avoided being struck by the car behind. People appeared in nearby buildings and stared at the blinding display of light and sound, the placement allowing those in the street a full view of the letters inscribed in lights.

"It's a message!" Marta cried, her voice barely audible over the shrieking fireworks.

More explosions appeared on the barrier, the lights gradually shaping into words. Every firework had been intentionally placed so as to contribute to the message, collectively forming an invitation in sparks and fire.

BE MY DATE 4 THE 4TH?

The question mark appeared in sparklers that ignited several mortars at once. They ignited together, bursting and exploding in a vivid tapestry of colors against the velvet backdrop of the night sky. Cars had stopped completely, their drivers and passengers audibly praising the unexpected celebration. Someone began to clap and it spread, until drivers, passengers, individuals in the store across the street, and patrons from Marta's restaurant were all outside, applauding the invite.

Kate stood in the midst, her heart bursting like the fireworks in the heavens. She realized his invitation had come late because of the effort required to make the board and link the fuses so they would go off in order. He'd planned it all. For her.

Although he'd planned with such detail before, she sensed an intention that had been absent on prior dates, as if he *wanted* her to know she mattered to him. He wanted to make tomorrow night special. Her assumption was mirrored by her roommates.

"It's about time," Ember breathed.

"You think he's ready?" Kate breathed, watching the fireworks gradually sputter into darkness and silence, their message delivered in their brief life.

"If he did this," Brittney said, "he's ready."

"Are you?" Marta asked.

Kate's smile almost broke her cheeks, causing her roommates to laugh and nod, all agreeing that Reed was finally ready to move forward. Reed, ever the romantic showman, was bringing their game to a brilliant, explosive close.

The last spinner died on the sign and the crowd reluctantly moved on, the drivers answering the honks from those who hadn't witnessed the display. They drove away, casting lingering looks back as if hoping to see more. Kate watched the final firework sputter and darken, her smile as bright as the invitation.

Three individuals appeared and stripped the fireworks from the sign, dropping them into buckets of water. All wore masks that covered their faces but Kate recognized one as Jackson. She thought one was Reed but she couldn't be sure. In remarkably short order they'd disposed of the spent fireworks and removed the sign.

Kate remained in place until the sign had been loaded onto Jackson's truck and driven away. Then her roommates finally dragged her back into the restaurant to eat, the meal dominated by speculation as to what Reed had planned.

Throughout the conversation Kate struggled to keep her anticipation from spilling into movement, and she fidgeted constantly. Her relationship with Reed felt old and seasoned, yet they had never once held hands or kissed. Despite the lack of intimacy she recalled every accidental touch, the brushing of his hand against hers, the lightning sparking in her body . . .

"I can't believe you haven't slept with him," Ember said.

Kate focused on Ember. "That's not our relationship."

"He hasn't even kissed you?" Marta's mother asked, returning with a dessert.

"I hope to remedy that tomorrow night," Kate said, and flushed like a teenage girl.

Her comment drew a round of teasing, and then Marta asked, "Do you think he'll want more than a kiss?"

Kate shook her head. "One wall at a time."

"A romantic man is a passionate man," Marta's mother said, drawing a gasp from Marta.

"Mother!"

She shrugged. "It's worth the wait." Then she turned to care for a couple that had just walked in.

Mortified, Marta shook her head. "This whole thing has drawn out a side of my mother I never knew."

"She's letting you date who you want, now," Brittney pointed out.

"True," Marta said. "But I've learned things about my parent's relationship that I can't un-know." She shuddered, eliciting a round of laughter.

117

"We should go," Ember said. "We need to start picking out Kate's outfit for tomorrow night."

"No jeans and a shirt?" Kate asked.

Ember cast her a scathing look. "The bigger the date, the more important the outfit. Honestly, how have you made it this far without us?"

Kate smiled, too excited to argue. "I couldn't have."

Ember pulled out her wallet. Although Marta's mother insisted no check, they always left a generous tip. Kate added cash to the pile and they departed, each pausing to embrace the large woman.

"Take care of the man you love," Marta's mother said.

"I don't love him," Kate said nervously.

Maria winked. "And my enchiladas are not the best in the city."

"They *are* the best in the city," Brittney said.

"Exactly," the woman said.

Uncertain how to respond, Kate said, "Thank you for dinner."

"I look forward to hearing about your date," Maria said over her shoulder, already heading to refill drinks for a table of seven.

They walked out into the parking lot and piled into Ember's jeep. As they drove home, Kate wondered if Marta's mother was right. Did she love him? They hadn't even kissed, so how could she love him?

She swallowed and nervously pushed the thought aside, unwilling to explore it until she knew Reed's intentions. They entered their house like an invading army, intent on vanquishing their closets. In minutes clothes were scattered across the living room and hanging over chairs, the remains of outfits deemed unworthy.

Kate dressed and undressed, trading clothes so they could be inspected, admired, and criticized by the blondes. The task would have been tedious, but she floated through the whirlwind of cloth on a cloud of euphoria.

Ultimately an outfit was selected and she stood before the full mirror in Ember's room, admiring the view. The jeans were Ember's, discarded and returned a dozen times until paired with Kate's own green top. The short sleeves had artistic cutouts that revealed a hint of her shoulders while the outfit hugged her torso and tied at her waist. It was a touch revealing yet reserved, a tease that enticed.

Marta had contributed a tasseled band that wrapped around her waist and accentuated her hips. Brittney, loathe to go without donating something to the ensemble, had contributed the earrings, small emerald studs that glittered in the light, a perfect pairing with her shirt and eyes.

"You look stunning," Ember said.

The other girls crowed with delight and Kate stared at herself, delighted with the results and grateful they had not tried to change her choice in shoes. They had insisted on her dark sneakers, the coloring allowing the focus to be on the green.

"You think he'll kiss me?" Kate asked, voicing her doubt.

"He'd be crazy not to," Marta said.

"He'd be stupid not to," Ember corrected.

Kate smiled at the stunning image in the mirror, wondering about tomorrow night. She felt fear and excitement, worry and hope, all blending into a cacophony of emotions that dried her throat and clogged her voice. But it was anticipation that came out on top.

"Looks like I'm ready," she said with a smile.

Chapter 3

The next night Kate dressed for her date and finished her makeup. The whole day, she'd vacillated between excitement and nervousness, and not even Brittney's white chocolate macadamia nut cookies had helped.

"You have it bad," Marta said from the door, savoring one of the remaining cookies.

"It feels like our first date ever," she said, checking her makeup for the hundredth time.

"Of course it feels like the first date," Marta scoffed, poking her head into view. "That's when most of us kiss."

"Or more," Ember called.

"Or less," Kate said, shaking her hands. "How can I be so nervous about kissing a guy? It's not like I'm going to spend the night with him."

"You've built this moment into a mountain," Brittney reasoned. "You just need to climb. We all know he's gorgeous."

"You think so?" Kate asked, glancing her way.

Brittney grinned. "He's better looking than Jason—and Jason was hot."

Kate laughed nervously and forced herself to step away from the mirror. Perhaps they were right, and she'd built up this moment until it seemed insurmountable. It was just a kiss, and he might not even come to that.

Had she over-thought the night? Had she assumed something that was not going to happen? Fear suddenly gripped her. But she jerked her head, discarding the thought with a rigid *No*, she was not imagining the depth of his feelings.

The doorbell rang and she flinched. Ember smirked as she saw Kate's nervousness and rose from the couch, beating Marta and Brittney to the door. When she swung it open, Reed stood framed in the doorway.

Dressed in jeans and a shirt bearing the United States flag, he looked much like he always had, but a twinkle in his eye sent a shiver down Kate's body. Without speaking a word, he seemed to call to her, and of its own accord, her body answered.

She advanced to greet him and he pulled her into an embrace, the contact soft yet firm. She breathed deep of his cologne, the scent mingling faintly with the cotton of his shirt, which hugged his shoulders as tightly as she did.

"Ready for tonight?" he asked.

Her heart jumped at the loaded question. "Ready for anything."

He laughed and waved to the blondes. "Thanks for not telling Kate about the firework sign."

Kate registered the comment and rounded on them, but all three looked shocked. Even Ember appeared surprised, and as she stuttered a protest Kate rotated back to Reed. He bore a smile of satisfaction.

"They didn't help me," he admitted. "Not for lack of trying, though. Ember was quite persistent with Jackson."

"Stubborn brute," Ember muttered.

"That he is," Reed said, and then gestured to his car. "I hope you're hungry."

"Starved," she said.

She abruptly realized she hadn't eaten anything besides Brittney's cookies. She'd been so distracted by Reed's date she'd forgotten food. She cast him a surreptitious look and found his eyes on her, a smile on his face.

Her roommates called out a farewell, their voices tinged with smiles, but Kate hardly noticed. She walked with Reed to his car and he opened the door for her. Then he got in and they drove away.

"I'm sorry the invite took so long," he said.

"You're worth the wait," she said, laughing nervously as she realized how her statement could be interpreted.

He grinned. "It took forever to set up the board, and it was hard to actually get the fireworks. We had to drive all over the city for the right ones."

"I can't believe it all worked," she said. "Once I saw the message I was worried something wouldn't fire on time."

"I was worried, too," he said. "So I watched it from down the street."

"It was a risky invite," she said. "A bold invite, but a risky one."

"I figured it was worth the risk," he said, his lips twitching with amusement.

She looked away so he wouldn't see her flush. In an effort to find a safe subject, she asked about dinner. After all the denials she expected him to refuse to answer, but to her surprise he did.

"We're doing a barbeque in the park," he said. "I have the smallest pavilion reserved in the Boulder City Park. We're doing a Build-a-Burger bar."

"Really?" she asked.

"Yep," he replied. "Can't go wrong with a good burger."

"Too true," she said.

A firework burst on a nearby street. Small and cheap, the spark of light faded under the light of the setting sun. The group of kids shouted in delight and set about lighting the fuse of another, and the screaming firework went off as they turned the corner.

"They should have waited," he said. "It's stupid to light the fuse before the right time. You rob the fireworks of their brilliance." He cast her a meaningful look.

Her skin tingled and she had to swallow. "It's almost dark," she said. "So it's almost time."

They shared a smile and then he turned onto the freeway that would take them downtown. A few minutes later he pulled off and headed to a park overlooking the valley. Small pavilions dotted the slope, interspersed with tracts of trees and fields of grass. A sign as they entered the park indicated the city fireworks would start at nine.

"You're taking me to see the city fireworks?" she asked.

"You sound unimpressed."

She gestured to the thousands of cars threading into the parking spots along the way. "After everything else you've done, this just seems a little . . . easy?"

"I'm certainly not easy," he protested.

She laughed. "True."

"I think you'll be pleased with the evening," he said cryptically.

She threw him a look but he merely smiled and turned up a small side road. The main road through the park branched into dozens of smaller roads, each leading to pavilions scattered throughout the park. Most were large enough for a group, but a handful were no more than a table and a barbeque stand. Reed's destination sat at the top of the park, a refuge hidden in a stand of trees.

She exited the car and breathed deep of the warm air, the scent tinged with pine and stone. Below, people were setting up chairs and blankets to view the fireworks. Children ran about with sparklers in hand, the festive atmosphere filled with laughter and music.

Reed unloaded a cooler and several boxes, which he set out on the table. As he poured charcoal into the grill, she turned and joined him, picking up the lighter on her way. He accepted it with a nod and set to lighting the charcoal.

123

"This is wonderful," she said, sweeping her hand at the vista.

"The night is young," he said. "But first, dinner. We'll have to wait for the charcoal to be ready, but you can lay out the toppings if you'd like. I asked Marta what you like and she gave some suggestions, but I brought some of my favorites as well."

She opened the cooler and began unloading the various potential toppings for the burger. Bacon, cheese, lettuce, and tomato were expected, as were pickles and various sauces, but there were several surprising options.

There were three cheeses including cheddar, pepper jack, and pimento. Avocado, sautéed mushrooms and onions, and a handful of onion rings were also available. Reed took the avocado from her hand and pulled a cutting board from the box.

"You don't mess around," she said, her tone filled with praise.

"I'm what you call a burger snob," he admitted. "I'm okay with most burgers, but I'm always on the hunt for a good one. I also prefer to have homemade fries, but those would be hard to cook in a park."

"Chips are good," she said, pulling them out of the box. Then she noticed an odd choice. "Pita chips?"

"Those are the appetizer," he said. "We'll dip them in Nutella." He pointed to the box and she spotted the jar.

"And dessert?" he asked.

"An all-American trifle," he said with a smile. "It's in the cooler."

She pulled it out and admired the multi-layered dessert, complete with pudding and various fruits. "You know, if you didn't have the dating thing down, you could get any girl with just your cooking."

"What if I don't want just any girl?" he asked with a teasing smile.

She met his gaze, her heart accelerated anew. "Then you could have the one you want," she said.

He smiled and nodded, returning to his work. She continued to unload the dinner but stole frequent glances in his direction. She'd thought herself confident before, but now she felt certain. And she yearned for the impending kiss.

Chapter 4

The conversation remained light and flirty, and she noticed he'd forsaken certain boundaries. As they prepared the meal together their hands frequently brushed, each contact sparking across her skin.

He shaped the hamburger with care and, when she admitted her brother had always insisted on managing the grill without her, showed her how to do the same. His easy smile appeared often as he helped her mold the meat into the right shape.

"If this was a pottery wheel it would be sexy," she said.

He burst into a laugh and pointed to the grill. "That should be about ready. You can throw them on."

The crowd had grown significantly as the sun set, with some setting their chairs and blankets on the opposite side of the road. Highly aware of the proximity, Kate glanced their way several times, and frowned when she noticed one of the women looking at Reed, a quizzical expression on her face.

The burgers finished and they each built their own, selecting the toppings like they were building a bomb. Amounts were measured and examined, and then added with great flair. Kate chose bacon, all three types of cheese, avocado and onions.

"I can't stand mushrooms," she said with a shudder.

"More for me," he said, plucking one and tossing it into his mouth.

They sat down to eat and she took the first bite, all but moaning as the flavors merged in her mouth. Noticing her expression, he grinned and bit into his own burger. She looked at the burger with new eyes, all the previous hunger flooding back. Then she bit again with equally tantalizing results.

He caught her glancing at the girl nearby and said, "What are you looking at?"

"She keeps looking at us," Kate said, subtly pointing at the girl. "She's the one in the blue flag shirt sitting next to the guy in the Broncos hoodie."

He glanced their way and frowned. "She looks familiar. Do you know her?"

She shook her head. "Not that I can recall. But she seems to be looking at you more than me."

Kate stole another look, and the girl rose to her feet, pulling her apparent boyfriend up with her. Then she turned and strode towards the pavilion, obviously intent on talking to them. Reed wiped his mouth on a napkin.

"It looks like we're going to find out."

The girl walked in, holding hands with her boyfriend. "Reed?" she asked.

He squinted in the dim light. The sun had almost gone down and only the lamp Reed had brought illuminated her face. She was undeniably beautiful, with bright red hair and blue eyes. Tall and slender, she had an athlete's build and graceful legs.

"Melissa?" Reed asked. He smiled and stepped forward to hug her. "I haven't seen you in what, two years? How have you been?"

"Great," she said, ending the brief contact. "This is Warren, my fiancé."

Kate offered her hand. "Kate."

Mellissa smiled and nodded to her. "Reed's dates are legendary."

"It's true," Warren said with a laugh. "You set the bar pretty high, you know."

"Sorry," Reed said, flashing his smile.

"Don't apologize," Melissa said. "You were the best thing that ever happened to me. You helped me see that dating was more than just hooking up. Because of you I learned how to find someone that really mattered to me."

"I can't take all the credit," Reed said. "How long have you been engaged?"

Warren and Melissa exchanged a look, the softness to the expression revealing the depth of their affection. "Three months," they said in unison, and Warren added, "but we dated for a year before that. She really put me through the paces, wanted to see if I was worth it."

"You were," she said, nudging him.

He laughed. "Only after I learned how to treat a girl."

Melissa suddenly seemed to notice Kate standing awkwardly nearby. "Sorry to interrupt your date," she said sincerely. "I just never got a chance to thank him. Reed changed my life."

"I think that's a bit of an exaggeration." Reed laughed but it sounded strained.

"It isn't," she said. "But anyway, I just wanted to thank you." She looked to Kate and nodded. "He's the best. Enjoy your night."

"I will," Kate said.

"Enjoy the fireworks," Warren said as they walked away.

Reed chuckled under his breath after they left. "Was that as awkward for me as it was for you?"

"No," she said, resuming her seat. "It was worse for me."

He grimaced. "I'm sorry," he said. "I didn't realize I'd had such an impact on her."

"When did you date her?"

"My junior year," he said. "Fall, I think. She really liked our first date and wanted a second. I asked her again but after that I was too busy, so I didn't ask her a third time. I haven't seen her since."

They sat in silence and she picked up her burger, which seemed to have lost its flavor. As she chewed she tried to identify what about the encounter set her on edge. Melissa had clearly been sincere. Warren too seemed genuinely grateful for Reed, as if Reed had personally introduced them and was the sole reason they'd fallen in love.

So why was she uneasy? Kate struggled to identify what she felt, her eyes ultimately settling on Reed. He seemed conflicted, the previous peace shattered after the conversation with Melissa. Perhaps what made her uneasy was not the conversation itself, but the impact it had on him.

"Everything okay?" she asked.

He smiled, but his easy smile was not so easy. "Of course. Care for more chips?"

She took some and added them to her plate. The previous euphoria had cooled. She ate but wracked her brain for a way to discard the intrusion and get back to where they had been earlier in the date.

"What's your favorite date we've been on?" she asked, attempting to steer the conversation back to them.

"That I've done or that you've done?"

"Either," she said.

"Ember's polls still say the people like the island date," he said.

"And you?"

"I think our first," he said. "You were the most beautiful interrogator I'd ever met."

She smiled. "I did ask you a lot of questions."

"That's an understatement," he said. "You wanted to know everything about me."

They laughed together and the tension seemed to ease, but Kate noticed a shadow to Reed's eyes. Several times she caught him glancing at Melissa, and despite Kate's best efforts, she couldn't regain his whole attention.

Her worries gradually mounted throughout the meal, and by the time they finished eating she had to force a smile. Melissa's appearance had shaken Reed, and Kate could not say why. Shortly after they finished eating Reed looked at his watch.

"The fireworks will start soon," he said. "We need to get going."

"Going?" she asked. "Are we not watching the fireworks?"

He shook his head, a sly smile on his face. "We're not *watching* the fireworks. We're lighting them."

Chapter 5

"No," Kate breathed. "Really?"

He grinned as he carried the cooler to the car. When he opened the trunk he unrolled a package containing two tags, each bearing the lettering, **Official Pyro Team of Boulder**. She frowned and looked up at him.

"Are we sneaking in to help with the fireworks?" she asked, and then raised an eyebrow. "Is this going to get me arrested?"

His smile widened and he shook his head. "A friend of a friend is a manager on the crew. He said we could help light the fireworks."

"A friend of a friend?" she asked, glancing at Melissa.

"A father of a girl I dated," he replied. "To be honest, I think he liked me more than she did. She wasn't into the creative dating thing. When I said we weren't going to a bar she lost interest."

"No wonder her dad liked you," Kate said.

They finished loading everything into the car and donned the tags. Then they climbed into the car and drove away. Kate noticed Melissa waving as they departed, and she reluctantly returned the gesture. The girl seemed nice enough and was clearly happy, but Kate didn't like the impact her appearance had had on Reed. Although conversation during the next part of the date had returned him to his previous demeanor, a shadow still tinged his eyes.

"Have you ever done this with another girl?" she asked.

"Never," he replied, and feigned hurt. "And if you'll recall, I promised I wouldn't do a repeat date with you."

"True," she said.

She smiled but his attention was on the road, which had narrowed considerably. They pulled onto the road and wound their way through the hundreds of cars and barbeques going on in the park. Families talked and laughed while children scampered about, chasing each other until parents called their names.

Dusk settled on the park, the darkness broken by twinkling stars. Lanterns glowed to life, illuminating families sitting around tables. Flashlights bobbed as people walked along paths between the trees.

Reed followed the road to the end and turned down a side road. Bordered by tall trees, the road led to a group of sheds placed out of view from the park. A group of shadowy figures were loading a pair of trailers with final supplies, and one truck pulled away as they entered the lot.

Reed parked next to the other vehicles and they got out. Reed fished a flashlight from his pocket and handed it to her and then clicked his own, allowing them to follow the path to the remaining truck.

"Reed?" a man asked.

"I'm here," Reed said.

The man rubbed his hand across his bald head. Then he smiled at Reed and offered his hand to Kate, a grip that nearly crushed her fingers. His kind eyes seemed to bore into her until he nodded.

"I hope you're ready," he said. "We got twice as many fireworks as last year."

"Ready as I'll ever be," Kate said, a thread of excitement warming her gut.

"Then let's go," he said. "Hop in and I'll take you there."

He stabbed a finger at the trailer, where two other men were already seated, the cab of the truck having already been filled. Kate exchanged a look with Reed, who seemed amused at the prospect of riding on the trailer, and then they climbed on, gripping the side supports for stability.

The trailer smelled of cut grass and was littered with dry clippings, repurposed from a lawn maintenance crew. Large boxes of fireworks filled the trailer and the truck, and showed dozens of glaring warnings.

Only to be operated by trained professionals.

Kate gestured to it. "Is that us?"

"It is tonight," Reed said with a grin.

"Don't mind that none." A young man, who couldn't have been over fifteen, waved dismissively. "We ain't got training and none of us been burned."

The truck revved to life and the trailer jostled forward. Kate reflexively grabbed one of the posts on the side of the trailer for support, but her body bounced into Reed. He reached out and caught her, holding her fast.

"I got you," he said, and then smiled.

She made no move to escape. "You think?"

"I do," he replied.

She smiled up at him, wondering if the shadow from earlier was just her imagination. In the red of the brake lights she couldn't see enough to be sure, but it seemed he'd moved past whatever had affected him from Melissa's visit.

The truck wound its way through a small, gravel road, the wheels bouncing over ruts, forcing her to cling to Reed for support. She wrapped her arm around his waist and held on, suddenly grateful for whoever had invented the trailer.

Not five minutes after leaving the sheds the truck exited the trees and pulled onto a wide grassy area behind a stage. Filled with equipment and speakers, the stage looked to be set up for a show, but only one person stood in front of a computer.

The truck came to a stop next to another and they got out, beginning to unload. Jim directed them to place the mortars a short distance apart, traffic cones indicating where they should go. With seven men and women already there, they finished setting up in just twenty minutes. Then Jim gathered them all to the trucks.

"Be safe," he said, "and don't be stupid. I'm talking to you, Ricky."

"I'm not going to do what I did last year," the youth from their truck protested.

Jim grunted in disbelief and then turned to Kate and Reed. "You two will stick together. Just light them throughout the music, but save six for the finale." He handed them each a long handled lighter. "And if it goes off on the ground, don't be near it."

"Are we lighting them in time with the music?" Kate asked, eliciting laughter and smirks.

"We aren't Denver," Ricky said, flicking his lighter on. "We don't need no electronics to light fireworks."

"We're here because we like to blow things up," another man said with a laugh.

Reed and Kate stood at their appointed spot and she looked up at the slope beyond the stage. Thousands of people gathered in a sea of color, all awaiting the coming spectacle. Sparklers ignited the scene as the music began to play, and a woman's voice sang America the Beautiful. Then Jim lit the first fuse.

Boom.

The mortar streaked into the sky and detonated in a blast of red and white, eliciting cries of delight from the crowd. Another mortar went off, and then another, the sky turning into a tapestry of sparks and light.

"Shall we?" Reed asked, raising his lighter.

"We shall," Kate said.

She stooped and lit her lighter. Then she touched the flame to the fuse and they hastily retreated. The mortar burst from the tube and flew into the sky, joining the cacophony of fireworks already exploding in the heavens.

"Your turn," she said, a wild grin on her face.

He stooped and lit another, and then she took her turn. Then they did two at once, laughing as they exploded in unison. Like excited kids, they worked together, lighting more and more, trying to keep up with Ricky, who was lighting fireworks nonstop, filling the grass with smoke and the scent of burned sulfur.

Smoke curled around them in a dense cloud, changing color as the lights blossomed in the sky, first green, then white, then blue and gold. The designated pyro crew were like wraiths in the smoke, their faces briefly illuminated by their lighters.

The music built, the crescendo rising to compel them to hurry, the lights providing a counterpoint to the music. Jim called for the finale and they rushed about, igniting every fuse. Then Reed and Kate stepped back as mortars blasted into the night.

The grass and trees filled with smoke and light, the heavens a brilliant display, crackling with sound and light. With the music reaching the pinnacle, Kate drifted closer to Reed, and when she looked at him his eyes were on her.

His fingers reached out and touched her wrist, the contact like lightning up her arm. It was warm but she shivered and drifted closer, watching the fireworks reflected in his eyes. His smile, always so easy and light, now betrayed a soft vulnerability that drew her in.

Her heart thumping in her chest, she slowly reached up and wrapped her arms around his neck, the motion tentative, worried. He tensed, doubt appearing on his gaze. He opened his mouth but she shook her head, a rare courage gripping her. Or maybe it was desire.

"I think it's time to stop pretending," she said, her voice husky.

In the midst of the fireworks and smoke, the music rising to the high note, she swallowed her fear and brushed her lips against his, sending electricity to her toes. She shivered and leaned in, yearning for more.

But he retreated.

Chapter 6

Reed leaned back, grimacing as if in pain. Kate stared at him, her emotions spinning like tires in the mud until suddenly they caught. Then her gut clenched and she stepped back, her hands falling to her side and balling into fists.

"Why did you bring me here tonight?" she said, her tone rigid.

"You know my rules."

"Don't give me that," she said, her hurt rapidly turning to anger. "We both know what you brought me here to say." She had to raise her voice to be heard over the fireworks and music.

"And what's that?"

"That you wanted to date me for real," she said. "No more games."

He opened his mouth to protest but no words escaped. Then his jaw clenched and he looked away, the conflict written on his face. The fireworks continued to ignite the night sky, but with each passing second her anger mounted.

"You don't understand," he said quietly.

"Is this about Melissa?" she demanded.

"No." he said, and then shook his head. "Yes."

"And Aura?"

"It has everything to do with her," he whispered.

"What happened?" she demanded.

He was silent for several seconds, the conflict twisting his expression. Anger bubbled inside her, rising to quell the previous desire, to bury it beneath a mountain of fury. But the desire remained, and she hated that her heart refused to break.

"I killed her." The words came out like they were forced from his lips, and he clenched his eyes against it. "I'm the reason she died."

"How?"

"She thought Tim would make her happy," he said. "But he was a human piece of trash that fell into a bottle. She didn't know how to leave, and one night they were driving home . . ."

He fell silent, the pain on his face finally breaking through her anger. She stared at him, at the agony he'd carried for so long, that he'd buried so none would know. She still didn't understand the cause, but she understood his regret.

"So this is your penance?" she asked, gesturing vaguely in Melissa's direction. "Help girls see that good guys exist?"

He nodded, the light of the last fireworks flickering on his face. "These girls that I've taken on a date, they start out thinking that all guys want is their body. They just want a guy to look at them, even when they know he doesn't care. I remind them that decent guys exist. I give them hope.

"Don't you see?" he continued, not even looking as the crowd cheered the finale. "Girls are stuck with these dogs and they're miserable. They pretend they're not, and hide their doubt and fear behind smiling pictures they post online."

"Jason was a good guy," she said.

"He was," he said, finally meeting her gaze. "But how many more are like him?"

She shook her head. "Not many. But this isn't a crusade that can be won."

"You saw Melissa," he said. "When I met her she'd just gotten out of a bad relationship. Her boyfriend beat her and thought it was funny when she bruised. When I dropped her off, it was like a light had sparked in her eyes, like she'd been *healed*."

137

"How long do you plan on doing this?" Kate asked.

She lowered her voice when she spotted Jim and the others collecting the mortar tubes. Kate and Reed had lit those at the front of the group, and for the moment they were out of earshot.

"Five thousand dates," he said.

Her eyes widened. "You can't be serious."

"One for every second I waited," he said.

She shook her head. "I don't understand."

"Eighty-three minutes," he said, his voice hard and clipped. "That's how long I was on the phone after the accident. That's how long I waited for an ambulance to arrive, until I heard the paramedic say she was gone."

"You were on the phone when it happened?" Her anger was gone, and his pain had become hers.

"She called because she was upset," he said. "Because he wouldn't let her drive."

"You heard the accident," she said slowly.

He stared into memory, his countenance broken, his shoulders hunched. Jim and the others hovered at the trucks, the cleanup finished, but none seemed inclined to interrupt them. Jim caught Kate's eye but she gave a tiny shake of her head. The man nodded and motioned to the others, and they piled into the second truck. He remained behind and folded his arms, obviously content to stay. The entire exchange went unnoticed by Reed, who stared at the departing crowd without seeing them.

"I heard metal crunch," he whispered, tears forming in his eyes. "I heard glass shatter and tires squeal. But most of all . . . I heard Aura scream."

Kate reached out to him and put her hand on his arm. He did not move or tense, and continued the story as if he didn't feel the touch.

"I shouted for her," he said. "I screamed for her but she didn't answer. I listened to her breath, to the rasp as she tried to speak. I told her I would call for help and used our house phone to call 911. I remember I dropped the phone and I cursed. I kept screaming for Aura but her breathing was weak. I just watched the clock while the lady on the phone said that paramedics were on their way. They were too late." He paused and looked to Kate. "*I* was too late."

"You couldn't have prevented it," she said.

"But I could have," he said bitterly. "I took her on one date and it wasn't good enough. I swore I would never make that mistake again. I couldn't make it right for her, but I could for others."

"Others like me?"

He finally looked to her. "Not like you. You've always been different. You've always been more."

"I cannot imagine what you've been through," Kate murmured, moving to stand in front of him. "But you can't fix the world on your own. Men will mistreat women and women will mistreat men. It's terrible, but it's how the world works."

"I don't want it to work that way."

"Then be with me," she said, putting her hand on his face. "Unless you're saying you don't want to be."

"I do," he whispered, his voice turning stricken. "But I can't. I have to finish what I started."

"I can't wait," she said softly. "You know what I feel for you, but I can't stand by while you show other women how they should be treated. Not anymore. Not when I feel for you the way I do. I know you're afraid, and I'm sorry for Aura—more than I can express—but I can't keep doing this, not when I know your heart is elsewhere."

She held her breath, afraid to make a sound. The seconds passed as she stared into his eyes, and for an instant she felt a spark of hope. Then he slowly shook his head, the tiny motion stabbing into her heart. Tears welled up and she turned away.

"Goodbye, Reed," she said, fighting to hold the dam. "I'll call Ember to come get me."

"Wait," he said.

He reached out for her but she was already walking away. She expected him to follow but the footsteps did not come, and the dam burst. Tears spilled down her cheeks as she disappeared into the smoke.

She cast a look back and saw him standing, his arm still outstretched, the conflict still on his face, tears also in his eyes. He did not call her name, and she did not turn back again. Silently sobbing, she left him behind.

She walked up the grassy hill where the people had stood watching the fireworks. Now she trod through their absence, not seeing the ground, not seeing the trees, not seeing what lay ahead. A branch blocked her path and she tripped, landing hard. Her hands filled with grass and she held the tenuous strands, fighting to stop the tears, but the effort was futile. She rolled into a sitting position and wrapped her hands around her knees, holding her legs as if the compression would stop her heart from shattering.

Alone in the dark, she cradled her knees and fought the regret, the anger, the pain. How could she have known what he'd endured? What he'd lost? She couldn't compete with Aura's memory, nor did she want to. Kate had dated guys that had driven home drunk, and she could have shared Aura's fate.

When the cold pierced the cloud of tears she shivered and wiped her eyes, suddenly aware that she was alone in the park. She felt a surge of fear, but it quickly faded. Despite their conversation, Reed would never have left her in the park alone. He was probably watching, unwilling to depart until she was safe. The thought only elicited more tears, and she struggled to pull out her phone and call Ember.

"Kate?" she asked. "Where are you? It's after one."

"I'm at the east park," she said.

Ember caught the tremble in her voice. "What happened?"

"I need you to come get me," she said, unable to stop the tears. "Please?"

For the first time in her life, Ember didn't argue. "I'm on my way," she said.

In surprisingly short time Ember's jeep pulled onto the road, the lights falling on her huddled form. Kate willed herself to rise but her body failed to respond, and a moment later three sets of arms picked her up and hurried her into the car.

The blondes fussed over her, but she sat mute and stiff. The tears were gone. Then Marta's voice managed to thread into her consciousness, her question piercing the din that buzzed in her thoughts.

"Where's Reed?" she asked softly.

"Gone," Kate said. "It's over."

Her roommates fell silent and Kate met their gaze. She'd thought her tears were gone, but they returned in a flood. Her roommates tried to console her, but their words were just a hum and she retreated into her mind.

"*It's over*," she whispered, the words echoing as she cried.

Volume 12: The Florida Date

Chapter 1

Reed watched Kate disappear into the smoke. He wanted to call her name, to call her back, to tell her he was wrong. But the words did not come. His heart felt stretched to the breaking point, like he was about to snap.

He wanted to be angry at Melissa for the reminder of his duty, but she did not deserve his ire. She was exactly what he wanted to see, a girl who knew what she deserved. But is that what he still wanted? Bowing his head, he rubbed his neck and trudged to Jim, still waiting at the truck.

Reed made his way to the passenger seat and climbed into the cab. Jim opened his door and joined him, inserting the key. He turned around on the grass and made his way back up the road, the truck bouncing over the ruts in the road.

"You shouldn't have let her go."

"You know my rules," Reed said. His voice sounded distant, unable to push through the numbness in his chest.

"Rules apply to a game," Jim said. "But your game is over."

Reed sighed. "I'm grateful for your help, Jim, but you don't understand."

The man grunted. "I've been watching the site—I've even voted on your dates. Don't kid yourself. You've fallen—hard. I may just be an old man, but I'm not blind yet. You shouldn't have let her go."

"It's too late now," Reed muttered. "She's gone."

"Everyone does stupid things," Jim said.

"So what am I supposed to do?" Reed demanded.

Jim didn't respond to his anger. "The only sane thing. I heard your story, so go back to the beginning. Resolve that burden you carry and then come back and get the girl you want."

Reed shook his head. "It's not that simple."

"It never is," Jim said, parking next to Reed's car.

"Thanks for the fireworks," Reed said.

"I expect an invite to the wedding," he said.

Reed shook his head and walked to his car. When he got in he drove up the road, but parked in a spot behind a pavilion. Kate had said she would call Ember but he wasn't about to let her sit in the park alone.

As he passed under a pavilion he spotted her in the empty field. His jaw tightened and he began to walk to her, intent on asking if he could drive her home. But he stopped on the threshold of the pavilion, struck by the despair about her huddled frame.

He could not offer solace or apology, and stood under the pavilion, unable to move. The minutes bled away as he watched her cry, yearning to offer comfort that he could not provide. If he went to her, he would beg forgiveness and give up his promise, but every time he tried to step forward he heard Aura's scream.

Kate's roommates arrived and spirited her away, their car disappearing into the night. Reed finally turned and trudged to his car. Then he drove home, the streets and lights blurring by until he found himself in his driveway. The light was on in the living room and he cringed at the prospect of talking to Jackson.

Steeling himself to face Jackson, he walked to the front door. He expected Jackson to already know what had happened and was not disappointed. When he entered the expression on Jackson's face said it all.

"Reed," he began.

"Not now," Reed said. "I'm tired, and I don't really want to talk."

Reed wanted to scream and shout, to cry, but the ache in his chest wouldn't allow it. Jackson was on his feet but Reed walked past him to his bedroom. He caught the handle and swung the door open, but before he could shut it, Jackson spoke.

"I'm sorry."

Reed finally looked at him. "Me too," he said.

He shut the door and fell onto his bed, but the war in his mind did not abate. Abruptly his anger boiled over and he punched his pillow, growling into it as if it would dispel the rending conflict in his soul.

Sleep finally claimed him, but when he rose in the morning he did not awake. Numb, he went to class and work, and returned home with notes he didn't remember taking. Time passed in a blur of faces. He ate when he was hungry and slept when he was tired, but more often than not he stared at his phone, at the last text he'd gotten from Kate.

His friends tried to talk to him but he extricated himself from conversations and escaped, leaving them wanting. After a week they stopped trying. After two they stopped talking. Only Jackson continued to make an effort.

The night of his date with Kate came and went and she did not text or call. The next morning he stared at the date on the calendar, a disturbing realization settling in like a fall frost. It was well and truly over.

The calendar marked dates with Kate for a couple months ahead and he ripped it from the wall. Tossing it into the trash, he dropped back in bed and pulled the covers over his head, trying to hide from the calendar.

The door swung open and Jackson appeared. "Get dressed," he said.

"Why?" His question was toneless.

"You promised to go to a game with me and Shelby," he said.

"I'm not feeling well," Reed said. "I'm going to stay in bed."

"It's the finals of the summer tournament," he said. "You promised you'd go with me, and I'm not disappointing Shelby."

Reed closed his eyes and groaned. He wanted to refuse his roommate but he had promised. "Give me a few minutes," he muttered.

He pulled on whatever clothes were handy and then walked to Jackson's car. From the passenger seat, he watched the streets slide by, the lights blending together in an endless array of bland structures until they were replaced with mountains. Then he realized they were no longer in the city.

"Where are we?" he asked, turning to look behind them, but there was only the road stretching to the horizon.

"On the 36," Jackson said, "about an hour from Denver."

"What?" he asked, straightening in his seat. "Aren't we going to the game?"

"The game was last week," he said. "You missed it. I'm sorry I lied, but it was the only way I could get you into the car."

Confusion cut through Reed's regret. "Where are we going?"

"Florida. Tallahassee to be exact."

"What?" he demanded. "That's two thousand miles away."

"I know," he said. "So I get credit for this forever."

"What are you talking about," Reed demanded. "Why do you want to drive across the country?"

"Because you need it," Jackson said. "And I'm a really good friend."

"Why do I need to go to Florida?" Reed asked.

"To see Aura," he replied.

Reed stared at him, his confusion spinning to a halt. "Turn around," he finally said.

"No."

"Now."

"No."

"If you don't turn around I'll . . ."

"What?" Jackson asked, incredulous. "Hit me? Unless you have a secret karate skill I don't know about, you'd better make yourself comfortable."

"When you stop for gas I'll just get out," he replied. "I'll take a bus back."

"Why?" Jackson asked. "What do you have to return to? Classes? A life? You sacrificed all your other dates because of Kate, your calendar is empty, and you just finished your summer semester. You got a B, by the way, because Ember talked to your professor."

"What?" he asked. "Why?"

"Because she's intimidating," Jackson said like it was obvious. "And we needed you not to flunk out."

Reed folded his arms. "I need to finish my degree."

Jackson glanced his way. "If you do your fall semester like you did the last two weeks, you'll be kicked out of school faster than I drive for a layup. Until you fix this, you've got nothing to go back to."

Reed wanted to argue but found he couldn't. Glaring at his roommate, he gestured to his clothes. "What are we supposed to do? Wear these clothes for two weeks?"

"Of course not," Jackson said with a snort. "Shelby and I packed your stuff when you were in class. Our bags are in the back."

Reed stared at his roommate, seeing him for the first time. "Who's the evil mastermind of this scheme?"

"I am," Jackson replied with a smirk. "Kate told them why you broke things off—."

"We weren't together—"

"—and everything about Aura. Since I was the first to know the truth I figured it was time to step up."

"And visiting her is going to fix things?"

"Yes," Jackson said.

Reed sighed. "Then there's a problem. She's not in Tallahassee."

Jackson raised an eyebrow. "That's where you grew up. I assumed she was buried there."

Reed sighed. "She's in southern Florida."

"They moved her body?"

"She's in a hospital outside of Miami," Reed said. "She's in a coma."

Chapter 2

Jackson stared at him until Reed reminded him he was driving. Then he jerked his head and returned his gaze to the road. "You said she was dead."

"I said she lost her life," Reed said, "not that she was dead."

"It's the same thing."

"But she could wake up—"

"No," Reed said flatly. "The doctors in Tallahassee *and* Miami were very clear. Aura is not waking up."

Jackson frowned. "You said it was your fault."

"She lost her life," Reed insisted. "And she lost it because of me."

"Don't you think you're blaming yourself a little too harshly?"

"No," he said, looking away. "And if you could still hear someone screaming as they died, you'd probably think the same thing."

"True," Jackson said. "But I'm not turning around. The destination may have changed but the trip hasn't."

"I don't want to see her," Reed said quietly.

"When's the last time you did?"

"Not since it happened," he said.

"You never visited?" he asked.

"No," Reed said. "So we'll drive for a week just so you can watch her parents throw me out."

"They're not going to throw us out," Jackson said.

"You don't know what her dad said," Reed said, looking out the window.

He lapsed into silence and Jackson eventually plugged in his phone and turned up the music. It seemed he made a point of avoiding love songs, but Reed didn't pay much attention. His thoughts drifted to Aura and he wondered how her family would feel when he walked in the door. He even considered calling but the thought of dialing the number was too daunting, so he didn't suggest it.

They drove throughout the day and into the night, only stopping for gas and food. At the first stop Jackson watched him like a hawk, but now that they were going, Reed sensed an inexorable pull to see Aura. Perhaps if he saw the girl he'd pledged years of his life to, he could recommit himself and try to forget Kate. If he even could.

They stopped for the night when they were tired and found a cheap hotel somewhere in Iowa. The next night they stopped in St. Louis. Reed frequently caught his roommate texting updates whenever they stopped. He offered to drive, but Jackson refused, claiming he didn't want to go back to Colorado.

"I'm not going to turn us around," Reed protested. "We've been driving for days. It would be pointless to try."

Jackson refused to relinquish the wheel, even when the sun set and they continued to drive. Reed kept to himself but occasionally allowed himself to be drawn into conversation that didn't relate to Aura or Kate.

It felt good to talk, but doing so was also strangely painful. Jackson had a way of finding amusement in the mundane, and several times Reed caught himself smiling. They reached Miami five days after departing and Jackson pulled into a Fairfield Inn. He paid for the room and dragged their luggage down the hall. Exhausted, Reed fell asleep in his clothes.

He awoke when Jackson flung open the drapes. "Time to go," he said.

Reed groaned. "I can't believe you dragged me down here."

"I'm your date for the weekend, remember?"

Reed lifted his head to look at Jackson, who was already dressed, lacing his shoes. "You're not as pretty as my last date." His jaw tightened as he thought of Kate but Jackson didn't notice.

"The breakfast ends in twenty minutes," Jackson said. "If you want to eat, you'd better hurry."

"And if I don't?"

"Then I'll bring you back a waffle."

The prospect of waffles pulled Reed from the bed and he dressed. The bag had been hastily packed but at least the clothes were his. He found shorts, pants, and a variety of shirts, some of which were absurd.

"My orange jersey?" he asked, holding it aloft.

"Never know when you're going to need to play," Jackson reasoned.

"So Shelby picked out most and you added a few?" Then he noticed a bright green shirt and held it aloft. "What's this?"

Jackson grinned and stood. "Kate's roommates also helped us pack. The blondes wanted to pick an outfit that was properly somber but would remind you of Kate."

"You regret telling them your plan to kidnap me," Reed guessed.

"So much," Jackson said fervently.

Reed pulled on his shoes and joined him at the door. They grabbed breakfast and returned to their room. Once they had everything packed, they checked out and loaded the car. As they left the parking lot Reed began to feel nervous.

"What if her parents throw me out?" Reed asked.

"You were her friend for what, ten years? They're not going to throw you out. They might not even be there."

"It's Wednesday," Reed said. "They'll be here."

151

"My apologies," Jackson said. "Next time I kidnap you I'll do it on a different day."

Reed chuckled in amusement but it came out nervous. He took a breath to steady himself and looked out the window, watching the cityscape of Miami gradually scroll by. He'd thought about what he would do if he ever came to see Aura, but now that the moment was upon him he couldn't think of what he would say.

Jackson followed the GPS to the hospital and found a parking spot. When he turned off the car they both sat in silence while Jackson waited expectantly. Reed realized Jackson had taken him as far as was going to and steeled himself for facing Aura.

"Let's go," he said.

He got out of the car and walked to the front doors of the hospital. A quick inquiry led them to the sixth floor. The elevator doors closed and Reed fidgeted in place, folding his arms and then putting them at his side repeatedly.

"Relax," Jackson said. "They'll be happy to see you."

"Her father told me if I had been faster calling 911 Aura would still be with them. He said it's my fault she's gone."

Jackson raised his eyebrow. "He really said that?"

"In the hospital three weeks after the accident," Reed said. "The doctors had just informed them that there was very little brain activity and to prepare for her passing."

"It's been three years," Jackson said uncertainly. "I'm sure he's forgiven you by now."

"We're about to find out," he said.

They exited the elevator into a small foyer. Chairs sat around a window, behind which a nurse worked at a computer. Hallways extended away, broken by beds and stands holding IV bags. A pair of nurses talked next to a drinking fountain while a handful of family members moved about. Everything about the floor was lethargic, reflecting the placard on the wall.

Long-Term Care

They stood outside the elevator until Reed realized Jackson was waiting for him, and a glance revealed Jackson's nervousness. He tried to hide it, but there was a stillness about his expression, about his stance, that betrayed his worry. He looked the same before a tip-off of a big game, except then he was also excited. At least then he knew what to do when the whistle blew.

Reed stepped to the receptionist and inquired where to go, and then walked down the hallway towards room 406. Thirty steps felt like an eternity, the hallway stretching away like a race track without a finish line.

He reached the door and slowed, listening for any sounds inside, but only heard the soft whirring of machines keeping someone alive. He swallowed, struggling to keep his emotions in check. Then he stepped through the door.

His shoe squeaked against the floor and he winced as if he would wake someone. A chair scraped against the floor and then Reed stepped around the curtain to see a man rising from a chair. Their eyes met, but Reed's gaze slid off his rigid features and settled on the woman in the bed.

Aura.

Chapter 3

She lay in bed with her arms at her side. She'd been in a coma for three years but looked good. Her features were a bit gaunt, but she was just as attractive as she'd always been. His gut tightened at seeing her in such a state.

"What are you doing here?" her father asked, his voice hard.

"I'm sorry," Reed said. "I just . . ."

"You should go," he said, coming around the bed and tossing his book onto the table. "You don't belong here."

"Who doesn't belong here?" a woman said, entering the room with a bottle of water.

She caught sight of Reed and Jackson and came to a halt. Short and sporting short white hair, she looked up at Reed in surprise, and then abruptly she smiled. She put the water down and pulled Reed into a crushing hug.

"It's about time you showed up."

Tears blossomed in Reed's eyes and he hugged her back, the embrace breaking the barrier in his heart. For several seconds he held onto the woman like she was a lifeboat and he was drowning. When they parted the man growled.

"Sheila," he said. "He did this to her."

"Harold," she said, "sit down before you have an aneurism."

He grunted and snatched his book before sitting down. Glaring at Reed, he folded his arms and muttered under his breath. Sheila turned her attention to Reed and offered them seats, which they accepted.

"This is Jackson," Reed said. "My roommate, and the one who dragged me down here."

"So he's the one to blame," Harold said with a grunt.

Sheila ignored him. "Thank you, Jackson. I always knew it would take a lot to get Reed to come back—especially after what Harold said to him."

Harold jutted his chin out. "He's the reason—"

"*Harold*," she snapped. "He listened to her die. He's suffered as much as we have."

He grunted and stood. "I'm getting some coffee," he said, and stomped out.

Sheila sighed, her eyes on his disappearing form. "It's been three years but he still blames himself, not that he'd admit it. He's not really mad at you, Reed."

"I deserve my share of the blame," Reed said.

Her eyes settled on him. "A drunk driver deserves the blame—all of it."

"But I—"

"Did everything you could," she finished with a nod. "Without you, she wouldn't be alive. She frowned. "The doctors may disagree on that point. They say she's dead already and want us to pull the plug. Of course, they don't use those words. They say things like 'very little brain activity' and 'chances of waking up are astronomically small' and all that. Doesn't make a difference. She's still breathing so we keep praying."

"I expected her to be thinner," Reed said.

"Most coma patients gradually lose muscle mass, so when they do wake up they can't move very well. The doctors here are using some sort of muscle stimulation to keep Aura in shape. I don't know anything about it, it's all doctor speak to me. They might as well be speaking Greek. But at least she seems to be doing better." She picked up a set of

155

crotchet needles and returned to the project she'd been working on. "It's good to have you here."

"Can she hear us?" Reed asked, his eyes on Aura.

"The doctors say no," she said. "But I think she can." She reached out and patted Aura's arm. "Don't you agree?"

Aura didn't move, but Sheila smiled anyway. Reed and Jackson exchanged a look and Jackson shrugged. Reed wasn't sure of what to say so he stayed silent. Content to sit, Sheila continued to work, the crochet needles clacking.

"How often do you come to the hospital?" Jackson asked.

"Every day," she said. "Harold works on the weekends now. You should have come on the weekend to avoid him." She laughed to herself and Reed and Jackson grinned at each other, the comment easing the tension.

"It's good to see her," Reed said.

"She'd be happy you came," Sheila said, and then looked to Jackson. "Reed's house was just five houses apart from ours. Did he tell you that?"

"He didn't," Jackson said, and then glared at Reed. "He didn't even tell me the whole story until a few weeks ago."

"Can't blame him for that," she said. "After what he went through, I can understand why he doesn't talk about it. But Reed and Aura were like two peas in a pod for more than ten years. They did everything together, spent every minute side by side. But it wasn't until they were oh, sixteen? Then he started to like her for real."

"You knew?" Reed asked.

Sheila laughed. "I always knew. You didn't act on it, of course. You were afraid it would change your friendship. You didn't ask her on a date until it was too late, and she was already dating Tim. Of course, this was before Reed changed, before he figured out how to date."

"How do you know how I date?" Reed asked.

"I keep in touch with your mother," Sheila said, a sly smile flashing across her face. "But if that wasn't enough, I've been watching the website of your dating life with Kate. You make a good couple."

Reed looked to Jackson, but he shrugged helplessly. Reed wondered how he could have forgotten Sheila's intelligence. She may have looked like a grandmother, but he'd been a professor of psychology until Aura's accident, when she'd retired.

"My favorite was the color war," Jackson said. "I've already signed up for next year."

The needles stopped clacking. "You're the Jackson mentioned in the posts. You've done good work, especially bringing him to Miami. Reed needs to get over Aura so he can be with Kate."

"What?" Reed asked. "You *want* me to be with Kate?"

"Of course," she said, resuming her crochet. "You can't very well wait for my daughter. She might never wake up." She patted her daughter's leg. "I don't mean it dear. I know you'll wake up."

"I don't understand," Reed said.

She lifted her project and examined it for flaws. "You've carried your crusade long enough. It's time to let her go."

Harold shuffled back into the room and sank into the seat like he wanted to punish it. Then he unfolded a sandwich and began to eat, his eyes never leaving Reed. The seconds ticked by but Reed did not look away.

"I'm sorry," Reed murmured.

Harold wiped his mouth with a napkin and put the sandwich on the bed.

"Not on the bed, dear."

He picked it up with a scowl and moved it to the table.

"You should have called faster," he said. "They would have been able to—"

"No they wouldn't," she hummed.

"Woman, will you let me speak?"

"No," she said firmly. "This boy has been hurting just like you and me. He doesn't deserve your anger. He deserves an apology."

"You want me to *apologize?*"

"Yes."

Harold's frown deepened and he looked out the window. Reed opened his mouth to say the man didn't need to apologize, but Sheila's eyes flashed dangerously. He shut his mouth. Jackson hid a smile.

"I shouldn't have to . . ." Harold began, and then growled and stabbed a finger at him. "You know what . . ." he shook his head. The seconds passed until he looked to his wife and she nodded. Then he seemed to wilt. "I'm sorry," he mumbled, the muscles spasming in his face.

Tears formed in his eyes and he wiped his face in shame. Then he turned to the bed and wound his fingers into Aura's hand, more tears flowing down his cheeks. In silence, he cried, all the while massaging her hand.

"I'm so sorry . . ."

Reed stood and moved to him. Unable to speak, he put his hand on the man's shoulder. He expected Harold to shrug him off or lash out, but he stared at Aura until he wiped his eyes. Then abruptly Harold stood and wrapped his arms around Reed, holding him like he wanted to crush the life from his lungs.

"Thank you," he whispered. *"Thank you for saving my girl."*

The room blurred through new tears. The emotions Reed had buried for years burst from his chest and he hugged Aura's father, yearning to fix what had happened yet knowing it could not be fixed.

Abruptly the man pulled away and sniffled. He wiped his eyes with the back of his sleeve and then clapped Reed on his shoulder. Beyond him, Sheila rose to her feet and folded her project neatly.

"Now isn't that better?" she asked.

Harold didn't answer, but he met Reed's gaze and nodded. Sheila came around the bed and took Harold's hand, pulling him towards the door. He didn't resist, and followed her past Jackson. Then he seemed to realize what was happening.

"Where are we going?"

"Time to leave," Sheila said. "Let's go to lunch."

"I already have a sandwich," he said, gesturing to it.

"I know," Sheila said. "But we need to go."

"Why?" Harold asked, taking another step towards the door.

"Don't you see?" she asked, meeting Reed's gaze and offering a small nod. "He's here to say goodbye."

Chapter 4

Harold met Reed's gaze and then turned and walked out. With a final nod, Sheila departed, leaving Reed and Jackson alone in the room. After a moment's hesitation, Jackson stood and walked to the door.

"Jackson?" Reed asked.

He smiled and gestured to Aura. "I brought you this far, but I think you need to finish on your own."

"What am I supposed to do?"

"Talk to her," Jackson said. Then he walked out and shut the door.

Reed stared at the barrier, afraid to look at Aura. It seemed stupid to talk to an unconscious person but words bubbled up, the words he'd been afraid to speak, the words that had swollen in his chest.

"I should have come sooner," he said softly.

Reed sighed and took Sheila's chair, shifting it so he could look at Aura. It had been three years since he'd seen her, and the last time she'd been in a hospital bed as well. After the accident he'd come to see her every day. Then the diagnosis had been given and Harold had threatened him if he ever returned.

Reed leaned back in the chair. "I met a girl," he said. "Her name is Kate and I really like her. You'd like that, if only because it meant I wasn't still in love with you." He grimaced and looked away. "But then, I never did tell you how I felt."

"I should have," he said. "When I took you on that date the moment came and I tried. But deep down I knew you didn't feel that way for me and I was a coward. I know you didn't want to hear it but I should have told you the truth. Then maybe you wouldn't be lying in that bed." He sighed, his thoughts drawn to the last time she'd been alive.

Three Years Earlier

Reed checked his hair in the mirror and then raced to his car, waving to his mom as he walked out the door. She hardly noticed his departure, her eyes glued to Dancing with the Stars like it was the moon landing. The Camry he'd had since high school groaned to life and he pulled onto the road.

He hadn't seen Aura in two years, not since he went to Colorado. He'd tried to catch her on previous trips, but she'd been off at her own school in Gainesville. This time he'd planned a day specifically for when she would be home, and convinced her to go on a date.

He rubbed his sweaty hands on his pants and looked in the mirror. Did it look like he was sweating? He cringed and turned on the AC, blasting it in an attempt to cool off. He'd hoped going to school in Boulder would help him move on, but his feelings had only grown in her absence. And the last few months she'd responded less and less to his calls.

The widening gap had been painful, but she wouldn't explain. Every time he asked what was going on she laughed it off and just said she was busy. It was a lie and they both knew it, but Reed didn't want to call her out. He didn't want the answer—at least not over the phone.

He pulled into Aura's parents' house and turned down the AC. Then he got out and walked to the door, irritated that he was already hot. He hoped she wouldn't notice his nervousness. Their friendship had always been easy, and acting like he was pining would sink him before he had the courage to speak.

He took a breath to steady his nerves and then knocked on the door. A moment later Harold swung the door open and smiled, motioning him inside. He called out to Sheila and she appeared in the doorway to the kitchen.

"Reed," she said, wiping her hands on a towel so she could give him a hug. "Where have you been?"

161

"Still in Boulder," he said. "Just classes and work, the usual."

"It's been too long," Harold said as Sheila stepped away. He offered his hand, which Reed accepted. "What are you doing tonight?"

"Dinner," he said. "Then a movie, I think. Is Galaxy Diner still her favorite?"

"It closed down a few months ago," Sheila said. "Didn't you hear?"

Reed's smile faded. "I didn't, actually."

"Take her somewhere nice," Harold said. "Maybe you can talk her out of dating that trashbag—"

"*Dad*," Aura said, appearing at the top of the stairwell. "You promised you wouldn't call him that."

They all turned and Reed sucked in his breath. Aura was radiant, with a sleek black shirt and blue jeans. Her blond hair was curled and hung down her cheeks, falling in ringlets onto her chest. She smiled at Reed, and he could have melted into the floor.

"Hey, Reed," she said, coming down the stairs. "It's been too long."

"Far too long," Reed agreed.

She opened her arms and he stepped into the embrace. The press of her body was soft and warm, and he breathed deep of the scent of her hair. How could it be so intoxicating after so long? How could it bring back so many memories?

They parted and stood awkwardly for a moment as Reed wracked his brain for something to say, but the power of speech had abandoned him. As he mentally cursed his weakness, Sheila picked up Aura's purse and handed it to her.

"What time will you be home?" she asked.

Aura shrugged. "Whenever. Reed and I have a lot to catch up on."

"That we do." Reed smiled, immensely grateful that words had returned to his lips.

Aura tucked her hair behind her ear and stepped to the door. "Goodnight!"

Reed nodded to them, but Harold's expression was almost a grimace. His gaze was on Aura's back, suggesting the animosity was not directed at him. Then Harold caught him looking and shook his head.

"Remember what I said," he muttered.

"Harold," Sheila said, swatting him with the towel. "Leave them be."

He grunted and shut the door. As Reed walked to the car he wondered what had set Harold on edge. Reed knew Aura was dating someone, but hadn't realized her family did not approve. They climbed into the car and Aura shifted in her seat to look at him.

"What?" he asked, turning the car on.

"You haven't changed a bit," she said. "Same car, same clothes. Even same hair."

"Is there a compliment hiding in there?" he asked. "And for the record, my clothes are new."

"You look good," she said with a smile.

"You look great," he said, causing her to laugh.

"Where are we going?" she asked.

"I was going to take you to Galaxy," he said. "But your parents said it shut down?"

"A few months ago," she said with a nod. "A lot's changed in the last two years, and every time I come back it seems more different."

"How about the Olive Garden?" he asked, voicing the first restaurant that came to mind.

"I'm always up for Italian."

"How are classes?" he asked.

As he drove into town they shared stories of classes and work, filling in the gaps of the last two years. Their friendship had always been perfect, and they talked about current and past events. As they passed old haunts they laughed about old stories.

Despite the closeness, Reed sensed a rift between them, an unspoken canyon that put them miles apart. He guessed it had to do with the guy she was dating, but she hadn't spoken of him, and he wondered if he could ask. He was nervous and hoped he wouldn't start sweating again. As he parked at the Olive Garden she smiled.

"Are you going to ask or not?"

"Ask what?"

"Who I'm dating."

"I am curious," he admitted.

She laughed lightly, the sound warming his chest. "His name is Tim."

"What's he like?"

"He's a good guy," she said.

She described him as a football player from Kansas, and talked about his looks and his smile. But Reed noticed she said little about his character, and her smile seemed a little forced. It was the same smile he'd given his mom when she'd asked how his class was going. He'd said good, but it was a lie.

"Are you happy?" he asked.

"I am," she said, and the fixed smile appeared.

Reed smiled as well, but it was one of hope. If Tim really was a trashbag, then Reed had a chance. He got out and hurried around to open her door. She opened it first and shut it, smiling at his effort.

"It's a date," he said. "Am I not supposed to open your door?"

She laughed. "I already have a boyfriend. I can't call this a date." Then she leaned in and kissed him on the cheek. "Even if it should be."

His hope soared.

Chapter 5

Their dinner was a trip down memory lane, each story eliciting laughter. Throughout the meal he watched her, gauging her reaction, trying to find the right time to tell her how he really felt. One opportunity came but his courage failed him.

"Do you remember when we met?" Reed asked, mentally cursing his weakness.

She smiled and wiped her mouth with her napkin. "Miss Perkins's classroom, third grade. We were paired with each other and began to draw. The desk became a casualty and she had to separate us."

He grinned, recalling that the artwork had sprawled across both desks. "I thought it was magnificent, but to this day I cannot recall what we were trying to draw."

"Principal Harrison," she said. "But we couldn't capture his belly. Miss Perkins did not find it as amusing as we did."

"How many classes did we have together?" he wondered aloud.

"A lot," she replied. "Third, fifth, and sixth grades in elementary school, and at least four in middle school."

"Don't forget gym."

She shuddered. "I hated that class."

"Everyone hates that class."

She conceded the point with a rueful nod. "We had English, American History, and Calculus in high school."

"I hated calculus."

"Everyone hates calculus," she said fervently, and they both laughed.

"Whatever happened to our teacher?" Reed asked. "I heard he got fired."

"They found pornography on his computer at school," she said. "My friend's sister was in his class and said one day he just disappeared, but news travels fast."

Reed shook his head in disgust. "I hated the subject, but he made the math fun."

"Turns out he was just a creepy old man," she said.

Uncomfortable with the turn in conversation, Reed steered the topic back to their time together. But as they were waiting for the check she abruptly leaned forward and interrupted him.

"Do you mind if we talk about my boyfriend?"

His heart sank but he gamely nodded. "Of course."

She looked out the window. It had grown dark during their conversation and the street was filled with cars passing the restaurant, their headlights flashing and then dimming. Saturday night had brought people out in droves, and students converged on the bars nearby.

"He was nice at first," she said. "But he really likes to drink."

"Has he hit you?" he asked, alarmed.

"No," she said hastily. "But I get the feeling he has to restrain the impulse."

You should be with me!

He kept the words in check, but they reverberated inside his skull as they talked about Tim, how he'd grown increasingly physical in the last few months. She still really liked him, especially when he was sober.

"He's graduating this year," she said. "And he wants me to go with him to New York. He wants to go to NYU to become an attorney like his dad."

167

"Are you going with him?" Reed asked, trying to keep his voice neutral.

"I don't know," she said. "I think I love him."

"But he drinks too much."

"He's in college," she said. "Everyone drinks too much." She pulled out her phone and typed a text. Then she looked up at him. "I'm sorry. I forgot about your dad."

Reed played with his fork, trying not to think of his dad's drinking problem. "He's in AA now so he's getting better. He even met someone."

She reached out and covered his hand with hers. "I'm sorry," she repeated.

"It's okay," he replied, and managed a smile. "I'm probably going to switch roommates in the fall because Willis is doing the same thing. He stumbles in most nights and falls on the floor."

"Sounds like Tim," she replied.

They shared a sad smile and then the check came. Reed snatched it and paid, and then they left. On the way out he spotted a sign for the capitol building observatory, which was open late for today and tomorrow. He considered inviting her to go but decided it would be better to play it safe.

"Let's go to a movie," he said.

"Okay," she said.

They drove to the movie theater but most of the drive she was engrossed with her phone, texting furiously. Her expression grew more worried and when he parked in front of the theater she turned to him.

"Actually, can we go another time?" she asked. "Tim wants to come pick me up. He doesn't like that we are out together."

"He's here?"

"He drove us up from Gainesville," she said uneasily. "He has some friends at Florida State and they wanted to get together."

"Can he not pick you up after the movie?"

She bit her lip. "I'm sorry. He's already on his way."

The entire night shrank into a few minutes, and Reed realized he didn't have time to say what he needed to say. He swallowed, his mouth suddenly dry. A new text came and she looked at her phone.

"He's pulling in," she said. "It's been fun to catch up. Can we get together again?"

She reached for the handle but he caught her arm. "Aura," he said, forcing himself to speak. "Can you wait a minute?"

"What?" she asked, the earnestness in his voice finally causing her to meet his gaze.

"I just . . . wanted to talk to you."

"About what?"

"About what I feel for you," he said.

Her eyebrows pulled together and she swiveled in her seat. "Reed, what are you talking about?"

He looked away and then back to her. Then down at his lap. Then back to her. Why were his hands suddenly sweaty? He realized he was fidgeting and she was staring and a car was swerving into the lot. Then suddenly the words tumbled from his lips.

"Aura," he began. "I've actually felt this way for a few years, ever since you were in the choir and I watched you sing. Something changed and I looked at you differently, saw you for how beautiful you truly were. I was afraid to speak before but can't wait any longer. I think I'm in—"

Aura leaned into a kiss, the contact robbing him of speech. It was less than a second but it seemed to linger for decades, his heart soaring. Then she pulled away and he saw the apology on her expression.

"You're my best friend," she said. "And I'll always love you in that way."

His hope shattered, his heart bleeding into his feet. "Aura," he said.

"I'm sorry," she said.

She hesitated and it seemed she wanted to say more. Then her phone buzzed and she got out. Numb, he did as well, and came around the car as a black Camaro came to a halt. Tim leaned over and shouted through the open window.

"Let's go, Aura," he called, his speech slurred. "We're going to the gulf coast for a bonfire."

"One second," she said.

"Aura," Reed said. "He's clearly been drinking. Let me at least take you home."

"He'll be fine," she said, but her tone was filled with doubt.

Tim honked and called her name, which came out distorted. "*Aura!*"

"Please," Reed said. "Please stay with me."

She remained in place, glancing between Reed's outstretched hand and Tim's car. For a split second he dared to hope, and imagined her turning away from Tim and taking his hand. Her fingers even twitched. Then Tim honked again and she cringed.

"I'd better go with him," she said. "I'll keep him from getting hurt."

She took a step towards the car and Reed caught up, making a last, desperate effort. "Are you telling me you feel nothing for me?"

She stared at him, her blue eyes bright with worry and regret. She stepped to him and wrapped her arms around his shoulders, clinging to him as if he were an anchor that would hold her safe.

"I know you're good for me," she said in his ear, "but I want more out of life."

170

Stung, he retreated. She grimaced and tried to apologize but he retreated another step. She apologized again and then strode to Tim's car. Before the door had even shut he gunned it, nearly clipping a truck as he sped around the corner. Reed watched the car disappear around the corner, the bitterness like bile on his tongue.

It was the last time he saw her alive.

Chapter 6

Reed fell silent and looked to Aura. "I should have told you I loved you," he said. "Maybe then you wouldn't have stayed with him." He reached out and took her hand.

"I told you about Kate. What I didn't say is that she helped me move forward. She helped me realize I was okay. You'll always be a part of me. It just won't be the dominant part. It may have taken me three years, but I finally heard you. We are friends and always will be."

He stood and leaned forward to kiss her on the forehead. "Goodbye, Aura."

Squeezing her hand, he took the long walk towards the door. With every step a fragment of weight fell off his shoulders, and by the time he reached the door he felt free. He looked back and marveled that his link to Aura was gone.

He stepped out the door to find Jackson, Harold, and Sheila sitting around a table in the hall. Cards and money were piled in the center. All three looked up at his appearance, and Reed raised an eyebrow.

"We got bored," Jackson said.

"So you played poker?" Reed asked.

"At least we still have our clothes on," Harold said.

Jackson stabbed a finger at Sheila. "You could have warned me she's a hustler."

"Me?" Sheila asked innocently. "It's not my fault you broadcast your cards on your face."

Harold grunted and muttered, "It's your fault you read them."

"I fold," Jackson said with a sigh.

"And I win," Sheila said, a smug smile on her face as she raked in the money.

Harold threw down his cards in disgust. "How do you do that?"

"It's not the cards that matter," she said. "It's the people. I already know how to read Harold, and it didn't take long to figure out Jackson. Thanks for the money."

"You're welcome," Jackson said, and then looked to Reed. "On another, unrelated note, you might need to cover gas on the way home."

Reed laughed. "I'm sure I can cover it."

Sheila stood and caught a nurse's eye. "Judy," she called. "Thanks for letting us play in the hall."

The nurse waved dismissively and Harold dragged the table back to the wall. As Jackson returned the chairs, Sheila stepped to Reed and smiled up at him, looking for all the world like his own mother.

"Better?"

"Better," he said.

She smiled. "Thank you for the visit. You are welcome anytime."

Reed lowered his voice. "Will she wake up?"

"Only God knows," Sheila said, lowering her voice and glancing at Harold. "I think we've both come to accept that she's gone. But we don't voice it aloud. The doctors are always looking for a reason to let her die."

"I hope she does wake up," Reed said, embracing the woman.

"Goodbye, Reed," she said. "Take care of Kate."

"I will," he said.

He turned away from Reed to find Harold already there. The old man hugged him as well and then nodded before walking with his wife back into the room. Jackson joined Reed and they walked down the hall.

"You okay?" Jackson asked.

"Actually, I am," he said.

They stepped outside and Reed was surprised to find the sun setting. Had he really been talking to Aura all day? His stomach grumbled and he realized he hadn't eaten anything since the waffles at the Fairfield.

"I assume you'd like dinner?" Jackson asked.

"Anything but cold cereal," Reed said.

He laughed and they went out to eat. Reed paid. They climbed into Jackson's truck and started north, intent on getting in a few hours before stopping for the night. Throughout the drive Reed talked freely about Aura and Jackson listened. Reed had shared the details of the end, but now he shared the beginning.

"It's clear you were close for a long time," he said.

"She was there when my parents split up, when I nearly flunked trig, and even when we joined the chess club."

"You joined the chess club?"

"So I could meet a girl," Reed said.

Jackson had started to sip his soda and nearly spit it onto the steering wheel. "No, really?"

"Sara Granger," Reed said. "And she was gorgeous. The chess club roster quadrupled the year she decided to play. I had a crush like everyone else. It faded the next year when I began to see Aura differently."

"So you fell for Aura in what, the start of senior year?"

"It lasted three years," he said. "That's when she got in the accident and everything changed."

"Tim should have died in the accident."

"He was knocked out and didn't wake up until they were in the hospital," Reed said with a nod. "Only a broken bone and scrapes." Then he frowned, realizing he'd never talked about him. "How did you know?"

"Harold and Sheila shared while we played poker. They said he's now living in Texas going to school at a community college. He got a DUI from the accident, and has had another one since. Texas took his license."

"Really?"

"About time," Jackson said, his expression hardening.

Reed raised an eyebrow. "What's that about?"

Jackson glanced his way and then looked back at the road. "I've played sports my whole life and known plenty of athletes. Some like Tim are arrogant—especially when it comes to girls. They think if they're good at a game it gives them the right to dominate a woman. It doesn't."

Surprised at the vehemence in his voice, Reed shook his head. "I never thought about it."

Jackson laughed sourly. "My dad and I used to play in the driveway and he always said to leave the game on the court. In high school I was the star and it went to my head. Then I was in college and didn't quite have the skill to play on the school team. That's when his words began to sink in, and you rammed them home."

"What do you mean?"

"When we became roommates you had this whole idea about women that was new to me," Jackson said. "At first I thought you were nuts, but I watched the impact it had on the girls you dates. And it reminded me of what my dad had said. I liked the respect you had for women, and when I met Shelby, I swallowed my pride."

"You never told me that," Reed said.

Jackson shrugged. "I just want you to know that if you give up on your promise to Aura, there are others that will continue what you started."

"Are you worried about what I'm going to do with Kate?"

Jackson glanced his way. "Should I be?"

Their conversation had avoided Kate for the last two hundred miles, and Reed realized Jackson had done so by intention. But the mention of Kate sent a fire kindling in his belly. It had been there before, but the flames had battled with his regret for Aura. Now they burned bright and hot.

"I think it's time I get her back," Reed said. "If she'll have me."

Jackson laughed, the sound tinged with relief. "I'm glad to know we aren't driving ten days for nothing."

"You were right all along," Reed said. "I was falling for her. But I was afraid of what that meant. Do you think I'm too late?"

"I don't think so," Jackson said. "But you were in a funk for two weeks and by the time we get back it will be almost a month from your non-breakup at the Fourth of July."

"That means we'll be getting back right before it would have been my turn in the challenge."

A wide smile spread on Jackson's face. "You want to fix things with a date?"

Reed grimaced. "I know what I want. Should I call her now? Or wait for the date?"

"You might not be able to fix things over the phone," Jackson said. "You hurt her pretty bad. I think you need to do it in person. Do you know what you're going to do? It had better be epic."

Reed mulled it over and an idea came to mind. He'd thought of taking a girl to the event before, but it implied a significant commitment. Now? It was exactly what he needed. Excitement arced across his skin and a slow smile spread on his face.

"Trust me," Reed said with a smile. "It will be."

Volume 13: The Lantern Date

Chapter 1

Kate stared at her phone, trying to remember what Brittney had asked. Then she realized she'd asked for the date and she mumbled the answer. Was it really August 2nd? Four weeks since she'd ended things with Reed.

The passage of time had merged classes and work into an endless blur of faces. She vaguely recalled studying the night before for an upcoming exam, but the words were meaningless. She'd thought Reed would call but he hadn't, the lack of communication deepening the wound left by the Fourth of July. How had she been so wrong? But then, she could never have imagined Reed's past, and what he'd endured by losing Aura.

"*Kate.*"

She looked up, and her eyes focusing on Brittney. The girl's expression betrayed a trace of annoyance, and Kate realized she'd called her name several times. Then Kate looked down and saw the cookies on the plate. She accepted one with a nod of gratitude.

"Kate," Brittney said, "did you hear me?"

"Didn't you ask if I wanted a cookie?" Kate asked.

"No," Brittney said.

"Oh."

Kate turned her attention back to the kitchen counter where she was preparing her lunch. Brittney groaned and put the plate down. Then she grabbed Kate's shoulders, forcing her to meet her gaze. She gave a long, searching look before frowning.

"Kate," she said. "You need to get past this. You're like a zombie."

"I'm fine," Kate said mechanically.

Ember stepped into the room and took a cookie. "For someone who never dated the guy, you're certainly broken up that you're not dating him."

"He didn't want to date me," Kate said.

Ember waved the cookie like a sword, her eyes flashing. "Are you stupid?"

The insult needled past the fog and Kate frowned. "Of course not."

"Reed was falling in love with you," Ember said. "Don't you see that? Because *everyone* saw it. But you've spent four weeks wallowing like he abandoned you. He just had some things to work out. That's why he went to Florida."

Brittney threw her a warning look but Kate zeroed in on her roommate. "He what?"

"He went to see Aura's grave," Brittney said, her expression apologetic.

"When?" Kate demanded.

"Two weeks ago," Ember said. "He was in the same funk you were so Jackson kidnapped him."

Kate struggled to deal with the whirlwind of emotions. Had he really gone to Aura's grave? How long before he got back? Would he reaffirm his promise? Or say goodbye? The questions bombarded her, leaving her confused and hollow.

"We weren't supposed to tell you," Brittney said when she didn't respond.

"If something had changed," Kate finally said. "He would have called."

"Maybe he's still there," Brittney said.

Kate stuffed her hand into her pocket and yanked her phone out. Shoving it in Ember's face, she yelled, "He hasn't called or texted *in a month*. I feel terrible for what he went through, but if he wanted to be with me he would have done *something*. This is Reed we're talking about."

"Maybe he's trying to," Brittney said.

"What's that supposed to mean?" Kate demanded.

"Maybe he thinks this is what's best for you," she replied, glancing to Ember for support. "It's what happens in all the movies. 'I love you so much I have to leave' and all that."

"You don't leave the one you love unless they ask you to," Kate snapped.

Ember stared at her, her expression sad. "Leaving only benefits the person who leaves."

Kate folded her arms but couldn't stay still. The anger had burned away Kate's barrier of despair and she could not bring it back. Everything incited her to anger, even the cookie in her hand, which she realized she'd ground into minute particles.

"Reed is obviously still dealing with what happened to Aura and I want to help," Kate said. "Why won't he let me help?"

"You did say you couldn't wait for him," Brittney pointed out.

"*I'm* not the one with an issue," she snapped.

"But you were at one time," Ember said. "You hadn't gotten over Jason, remember? And Reed was there when you needed him. He didn't walk out when Jason appeared. He showed up the moment you called—without judgment."

Kate stabbed her finger at Ember. "Reed set up this whole date to kiss me and then he flinched like I had a disease. What was I supposed to do? Pretend like I didn't care? Because I did."

"Because you *do*," Ember said.

"Of course I do!" Kate shouted. "Could I have responded better? Maybe. But you try waiting five months for a guy to make a move only

181

to have him flinch. Maybe I should have heard him out, showed him that I cared . . . maybe I should have told him I would wait . . ." All at once her anger dissipated and she crumpled. "Please tell me I didn't push him away."

"You did," Ember said. "But that doesn't mean you can't get him back."

"Call him," Brittney said.

"I can't just call him," Kate said, wiping the tears from her eyes.

"Yes, you can," Ember said. "Or you can take my approach and show him how angry you are. But since he doesn't really deserve that, I'd suggest you go with a nicer option."

"You really think I can just call him?"

"*Yes*," they said in unison.

Brittney nodded. "If you don't, you'll regret it forever."

"How do you know?"

"Because it took you a year to get over Jason—and you didn't like him nearly this much."

"Not even close," Ember agreed.

The door opened and Marta came in. She'd picked up a morning shift for a sick cousin and was dressed in her uniform. Catching sight of the three of them in the kitchen, she walked over to join them.

"What's going on?"

"It's an intervention for Kate," Ember said.

"It's about time," Marta said fervently. "Is it working?"

"Hey!" Kate exclaimed.

"I love you," Marta said. "But you've been really messed up the last few weeks."

Kate grunted sourly, some of the last month flooding back, especially the night she was supposed to go on a date with Reed. Instead, she'd eaten Rocky Road until she'd passed out on the living room floor.

"I'm sorry I've been so depressed," Kate said. "Especially the night of my date with Reed."

"You needed to wallow," Brittney said. "But ice cream melted all over the couch."

Kate groaned and wiped a hand down her face. Then she realized her other hand still held the remains of Brittney's cookie and she stepped to the sink. As she washed the crumbs off her hands she watched the water flow into the drain.

"You didn't have to clean up after me," she said.

"At least it got us to clean the couch," Marta said. "It was getting disgusting."

"Amen," Brittney said.

Kate clenched her eyes shut and shook her head. "What am I supposed to do?" she asked, grateful for the sudden clarity of her thoughts and afraid it would not last. "Do you really think I should call him?"

"Yes," they all chorused.

Kate couldn't stop the smile. "Really? You don't think it's too late?"

Marta picked up a cookie and took a seat. "If he shoots you down, you'll know it's truly over. If he doesn't you'll get back together and be happy again."

"And if he shoots me down?" Kate asked, her stomach lurching at the prospect.

"Then Ember can break his fingers," Brittney said.

"You know I'll do it," she said.

"I don't think that's necessary," Kate said, allowing a small smile.

Kate took a seat at the table and picked up a cookie. The flavor helped steel her nerves, and abruptly she pulled out her phone. She fumbled to press the home button but her hands were shaking and she nearly dropped it.

"Put it on speaker," Marta urged.

They all crowded around the table as Kate complied, but her finger hovered over his name. He was still at the top of her favorites list. But her courage failed her and she looked to her roommates helplessly.

"I can't do it," she said.

"I can," Ember said. She stabbed the phone, her hand striking like a snake.

Kate tried to pick up the phone, but Brittney blocked her way. "It's already ringing," she said. "You can't hang up now, he'll know you called."

The phone rang three times, the sound reverberating off the walls of the silent kitchen. Kate closed her eyes after the second ring, shrinking at the prospect of him not picking up. Just as her heart crumpled there was a click.

"Kate," Reed said.

There was softness to his voice, as if he'd waited for her call for decades and the moment had finally come. She licked her suddenly dry lips, her thoughts tumbling through her head in a cacophony of voices. Should she be angry? Grateful? Worried? Her roommates frantically motioned for her to speak.

"Reed," she said, her voice a mixture of relief and tentative hope.

"I'm glad you called," Reed said, and she heard his easy smile in his voice.

"Really?" Kate asked. "It's been a while." A trace of anger tinged her words.

"I'm sorry about that," Reed said. "I really am. But I hope this will help you forgive me."

"What do you mean, this?"

The phone clicked off and all four of them stared at it. "Did he just hang up?" Brittney asked in shock.

"I'll kill him," Ember said. "Then I'll beat—"

The doorbell rang, and they all jumped. Then understanding washed over them and they scrambled for the door, Kate protesting loudly that she should be first. But Ember reached the door and pulled Brittney back so she could swing the door open. Reed wasn't there.

But his invitation was.

Chapter 2

A red balloon floated above a small bag. The breeze fluttered the balloon, making it bob and swing, the string tugging on the bag. Kate scanned the yard, but no one was in sight. Whoever had placed the pouch was already gone.

"I just talked to him," Kate said. "But he must have been already on his way here."

"You're asking that now?" Ember asked. "Open it."

Kate stooped and picked up the pouch. Glancing at the sunlit yard, she retreated indoors. Setting it on the table, she opened it with trembling fingers. Inside, a small card lay nestled in silk. Kate picked it up and read the note.

Kate,

Please forgive the marks, of a past now gone from sight.

Our last date ended with sparks, our next will end in light.

If you'll have me.

Kate stared at the words, her heart inflating like the balloon that hovered above her head. Questions and emotions flooded her in bursts of hope, doubt, and curiosity. How had he picked that exact moment to leave the invite? How had he made his decision? When?

Brittney cried out in excitement, causing them all to jump. "Sorry," she said. "I'm just excited."

Marta laughed. "Did you have to scare us?"

Ember folded her arms. "I don't like it. Why now? Why this moment?"

"I was wondering the same thing," Marta said.

"He always had excellent timing," Kate said, her smile turning soft.

"But aren't you curious?" Ember asked. "If he decided to ask you on another date, surely he knew before this moment."

"Perhaps," Kate said. "But I don't care. I'm just glad he's here."

"You think he wants to date for real?"

"This certainly sounds like he does," Kate said, holding the letter up to emphasize her point. "But I was certain last time too, and it didn't work out."

She frowned, her elation fading into worry. Abruptly she picked up her phone and pressed his name. Her roommates fell silent as she stood in their midst. She wasn't surprised when he picked up on the first ring.

"However did you manage the timing?" she asked.

"I've planned to invite you for a couple of days," he said. "You called as I was walking to your door. Nearly gave me a heart attack, by the way."

"What took you so long?" she dared to ask.

He paused, and she held her breath. "You were right," he said. "And I needed to figure out some things."

"And have you?"

"I have."

Her heart clattered against her ribs. "And the date?"

"You'll find out tomorrow night. I hope you can make it."

"I wouldn't be anywhere else."

"See you at 4:00," he said.

Kate hung up and stared at her phone. Then she turned to find her roommates on the verge of exploding. They'd huddled around her so all could hear the conversation. Then Ember shook her head.

"And just like that, you've forgiven him?"

Kate considered her response and then shrugged. "I have. He listened to Aura die, remember?"

"So, what do you expect out of this date?" Brittney asked.

"A kiss," Kate said, and then grinned. "And a boyfriend."

The previous elation burst across her and she grinned stupidly as her roommates celebrated. Marta snatched her phone and called Jackson, while Ember called Shelby. Brittney called Reed's mother, who Ember had called two months ago on Kate's behalf. In an hour the blondes had gathered all the information possible and the full story came out.

"Jackson and Reed got back two nights ago," Marta was saying. "Reed spent the entire drive planning this date, but Jackson refused to say what you're doing."

"Shelby concurs," Ember said. "But whatever it is, it's going to be outside. Jackson kept it to himself despite her best efforts to get him to talk."

"What about Reed's mom?" Kate asked.

Brittney stared at her phone like it was a foreign device, her silence quieting them all. Kate nudged her, and Brittney looked at them, her gaze focusing on Kate. Then she blinked and shook her head.

"Aura's not dead."

"What?" they asked in unison.

"She's in a coma," Brittney said. "I guess the doctors think she'll never wake up and want to take her off life support. Aura's parents have refused."

"She's alive?" Kate asked, stunned.

"Sort of," Brittney said uncertainly, and shared the events of Reed's visit to Miami.

"If she's breathing, she's alive," Ember said, folding her arms.

Brittney shook her head. "Machines breathe for her."

Ember scowled and looked away, and Marta gestured to the bag and balloon. "So Reed went to say goodbye to her and a week later he's on your doorstep?"

"I guess," Kate said uncertainly.

Suddenly overcome with the vacillating emotions, she sank into a seat, trying to come to terms with the volume of information. Remembering she still had the note, she lifted and read it to herself. Then she shook her head.

"He spent the last month trying to resolve his past," she said. "He wouldn't have left this note if hadn't done that."

"So, you're going to trust him?" Marta asked.

"I think so," Kate said slowly. "I know I want to be with him."

"Then you need to get ready," Brittney said.

"No," Kate said. "Last time we spent hours figuring out the perfect outfit. This time I get to wear what I want."

"Not even shopping?" Ember asked.

Kate's lips twitched. "Perhaps a little shopping."

Her roommates whisked her out of the house and into Ember's jeep, and less than an hour after the invitation they were in the mall, looking for tops. Most of their conversation was speculative, with even Kate wondering what Reed had in store for her. Several times she wondered about Aura, but the timing was not a coincidence.

The cold knot that had settled in her stomach when she'd first heard Aura's name had disappeared. Like an anchor had been cut, she felt as if she were floating on air. And her heart soared.

The whirlwind of shopping culminated in new clothes for all of them, and they returned to the house flush with excitement. Unable to sleep, they stayed up late, talking and eating a variety of desserts that Brittney concocted.

Brittney eventually fell asleep on the couch, as did Marta. With *The Notebook* playing on the TV, Kate sat curled up under a blanket while Ember sat beside her. They sipped on root beer floats and continued to talk.

"Do you think he's really resolved everything?" Kate finally asked.

"I think you're right," Ember said. "He wouldn't have asked you out if he hadn't."

"You think so?" Kate asked.

"Is it wrong that I'm jealous?" Ember asked.

"No," Kate said.

Ember gestured to the screen. "We're taught to hope for a fairytale guy that will show up and sweep us off our feet. I never thought I'd see it happen for real, and I guess I'm afraid it will never happen to me."

"At least we know decent guys exist," Kate said.

Ember shook her head. "I just wonder if there's a guy I won't drive away."

Her voice was uncharacteristically vulnerable, causing Kate to lean over and put her arm around the girl's shoulders. Ember didn't pull away, and instead released a mournful sigh before draining her drink.

"Your fire is what makes you attractive," Kate said. "And I suspect it will be what lands you the guy you truly want."

Ember laughed, the sound filled with rancor. "So far it's only gotten me a handful of restraining orders."

"I hope that Reed is my match," Kate said, "that we fit together. There's a match out there for you, I know it."

"I hope so," Ember said. "I don't want to think that Hollywood has lied just to make money."

"They've certainly done that," Kate said, stifling a laugh when Brittney twitched. "But that doesn't mean it's all false."

Ember yawned. "I hope you're right. Now that you've found your forever man I want mine."

"My forever man?" she asked, trying out the phrase. "Let's just start with tomorrow."

Ember laughed and patted her on the knee. "You keep telling yourself that."

She lay down and was asleep in seconds, leaving Kate to finish the movie alone. As the credits rolled she snagged the remote from where it had fallen next to Brittney's feet. She turned off the movie and stared at the blank screen, a smile forming on her face.

"Reed," she murmured. "I hope you're my forever man."

Chapter 3

Kate texted Reed throughout the following day, but the day seemed to drag forever. She teased and cajoled him, but he didn't give any more details than she'd already learned. They talked several times and he was frequently the one to call her, revealing he was just as eager as she was to be together. By the time he arrived at her door she was all set to grab his neck and plant a kiss.

She swung the door open the moment the doorbell rang, and there he stood. Dressed in a blue button up shirt and dark slacks, he carried a bouquet of roses. His black hair was perfectly combed, the stubble on his beard just begging to be scratched. He smiled.

"I believe it's customary to bring flowers with an apology?"

She took the flowers and invited him in, brushing his hand with her own. "What exactly are you apologizing for?" Her fingers tingled from the contact and she smiled.

"Silence," he said. "I should have called."

"I understand why you didn't," she said. "But I'm sure you can make it up to me."

"I intend to," Reed said, his lips twitching.

Her heart fluttered, and she grabbed her purse. "Ready when you are."

"Where are the blondes?" Reed asked, looking about the room as if he'd just realized they were absent.

"I banished them," she said. "They were becoming a nuisance."

Reed raised an eyebrow as they walked out. "A nuisance?"

"We were up pretty late last night," she said. "And they were getting cranky. I didn't want them bombarding you with questions."

"Painting nails and doing each other's hair?"

"That was part of it," she said.

Before she knew it, they were on the freeway headed south. She should have cared about where they were going but didn't, and caught herself examining his profile. With the sun setting, the light glowed on his features, illuminating his smile.

"I really am sorry about the last few weeks," he said.

"Want to talk about it?"

He glanced her way. "I'd gotten quite good at burying what had happened, and not even Jackson knew the truth about Aura. You made me look at things in a way I wasn't prepared for."

"I didn't mean to—"

"Don't," he said. "Don't apologize. Every date we went on forced me to face my guilt."

"How did it go in Florida?"

"I needed to see her," he said, glancing her way as if to gauge her reaction.

"And?"

"I may have loved her once," he said. "But not now. She's an old friend that will never wake up."

"You said she was dead."

"I said she lost her life. Isn't that the same thing?" He sighed. "Or maybe it was easier to just think of her as dead."

"What was it like to see her?"

"Strange," he said. "I used to feel so much for her. She was my tether for everything that mattered. There was nothing I didn't tell her, even what I ate for breakfast."

"And now?"

"My tether has shifted," he said with a smile.

She smiled in turn, and then said, "Will you tell me about her?"

"You really want to know?"

"I told you about Jason," she said. "It's only fair you tell me about Aura."

He consented with a nod and began to speak, telling her about his final date, and the call a week later where she'd gotten into the fateful car. Kate listened, grateful that when he spoke he spoke in the past tense, but also grateful for the insights into Reed's character.

Reed talked for an hour, the conversation shifting from amusing to serious and back, and Kate simply listened. Out of all the girls he'd dated, none had discovered what Reed kept hidden, because he had not allowed it. As he spoke of Aura he revealed his deepest vulnerability and she sensed a link being forged between them.

On impulse she brushed her hand against his, swallowing at the surge of emotion. He smiled and did not retreat, the back of their hands touching, the contact warm and exhilarating. She felt the urge for more but decided to wait. She was not about to rob him of this moment, not when he'd prepared with such care. As they pulled into Denver she perked up.

"Is dinner in our near future?"

"It is," Reed said, slowing as the traffic increased.

"Anywhere I would know about?"

"Not likely," he said. "But it's just a picnic in a park."

"Really?" she asked.

He laughed at the doubt in her tone. "Don't sound so suspicious. I thought it would be fun to drive down here because this park has such a stunning view."

"No views in Boulder?"

"Not like this one," he said.

He got off the freeway and aimed for a mountainside facing west. As they climbed through the trees the traffic was unusually dense, with many others ascending to the park. Then abruptly the trees parted and a plateau came into view.

With scattered trees and playgrounds, the park sloped gently downward. Small roads crisscrossed the tracts of grass and a huge crowd was setting up blankets and chairs. With the sun as a blazing backdrop, the view was stunning.

"It's beautiful," she said. "But it's rather busy. Don't you usually opt for seclusion?"

"Denver State had their finals this week," he said, "so I suspect there are a number of students up here. That and the local high schools start next week."

"Are you sure we aren't suddenly going to end up in a color war?" she asked.

He shook his head with a smile. "Not this time."

He nosed into a parking spot and they moved to the trunk, in which he'd packed an actual picnic basket, a blanket, and a large, wrapped gift. There were also two chairs, which Kate hefted while pointing at the present.

"Who's that for?"

"Myself," Reed said. "I thought I deserved something and went out and bought it."

She laughed and they began walking down the slope. He caught her attention as they passed a pavilion and pointed to an open spot in the center of the field. Still suspicious, she agreed, and they threaded their way through the picnickers.

"I still think you have something up your sleeve."

"Of course I do," he said. "You know me well."

When they reached the open spot, he unfolded the blanket and she unpacked the dinner, which proved to be a salad, sandwiches, and drinks. She inspected them with great care, wondering if the food hid the surprise. Then she saw the various wrapped packages in the bottom of the picnic basket.

"What are those?"

"Dessert," Reed said. She reached for one, but he caught her hand. "Not yet. You don't want to spoil the surprise, now do you?"

"I guess not," she said.

He pulled out forks and passed one to her. Then he opened the Tupperware with the salad and began to eat. She savored her own salad, but something was familiar about it. The dressing tasted exactly like . . .

"Is this Brittney's walnut ranch dressing?"

"You have a good tongue," Reed said.

"When did she make it?"

"I let each of your roommates, plus Jackson and Shelby, contribute to tonight's date. After all they had done, I thought it only fitting they got to be part of it."

"Did they know everything you were planning?"

Reed shook his head. "Jackson knew a little, but otherwise, I kept it to myself. All I said was that it was a picnic and watching the sunset."

Kate pointed to the basket. "I've seen that before."

"Marta's," Reed said. "And the blanket is Ember's. Which reminds me." He pulled out his phone and leaned close to her to snap a picture.

"Ember wanted a picture to post to the site. Apparently, it's gained quite the following."

"What did Jackson add?" she asked, eyeing the basket. Then she spotted two tiny boxes of cold cereal and laughed. "Are those from him?"

"He insisted," Reed said, shaking his head. "And how could I deny him?"

With delicious food and a breathtaking sunset, the dinner was near perfect, but the sheer volume of people in the park marred the moment. Reed seemed unperturbed, even when other families and couples placed their blankets close to their own. Although many were obviously there for dinner, there was a tangible mood of excitement about the people, as if they were waiting for an unspoken event. And as it got dark the excitement continued to build. She was about to ask, but as the sun set Reed pulled out a blindfold.

"Ready for dessert?"

"Why do I need a blindfold?"

"Because you have to identify the dessert by taste," he said.

"Is that necessary?" she asked, gesturing to the darkness.

He pulled out a lantern and flipped the switch. Other families also did the same and talked about the lanterns as if they were more than just lights. She frowned, but decided not to argue. She wrapped the blindfold around her head. When he was certain she could not see, Reed grabbed one of the packages and unwrapped it. She heard the paper fall away and a fork scrape a dish. She caught the scent of cheesecake and peanut butter. Then he caught her hand.

And held on.

Chapter 4

Energy crackled up her arm and into her heart. She swallowed at the sudden dryness in her throat, her breathing becoming labored as she felt his hand touch hers, exploring her fingers, and folding into her palm.

After six months of no physical contact, the touching of their hands—intentional and tender—filled her body with yearning. Every caress brought a shudder as his hand explored hers. He shifted to sit beside her, and his shoulder pressed against hers, causing a new world of sensations. She marveled at the power of his touch, as if all the resistance of six months had built this—holding hands—into the pinnacle of pleasure and excitement.

The intertwining of their fingers was tentative and intimate, the bridging of a gap that had become so enormous that to cross seemed impossible. She'd anticipated a kiss, but this was so much more, the culmination of suppressed desire suddenly exploding to the fore.

"What about your rules?" she managed to say.

"The game is over," he said, his voice soft, his breathing rapid. "No more rules."

"None?"

"Well," he amended. "Fewer rules."

"So, no sex?"

He laughed. "It took me six months before I held your hand."

Kate lifted Reed's hand and kissed his fingers, causing him to tense and laugh anew. She smiled, pleased that she'd managed to disconcert him. She wanted to look at him, to feel his gaze on her, but the blindfold provided a unique focus, and made the touch of their hands all the more electrifying.

"Ready for dessert?"

"I already had mine," she said smugly.

"Open your mouth," he said with a laugh. "Your job is to tell me what it is."

"Peanut butter cheesecake," she said.

"You haven't tasted it yet," he protested.

"I can smell it," she said. "And the smell of Brittney's cheesecake cannot be forgotten."

He placed the fork in her mouth and she savored the food. It had always been her favorite dish that Brittney made, but the sensations coming from her hand far surpassed it. She ran her thumb along his, feeling every contour and crease.

"Ready for the next?"

"Yes," she teased. "Whatever you have in store, I'm ready for."

He laughed lightly, and gave her another bite, which proved to be key lime pie, apparently of Shelby's make. She'd never really cared for key lime, but this particular pie was a perfect balance of sour and sweet.

For the next few minutes he fed her various pies, but the confections did not compare with the true dessert. The tingling of her arm did not diminish, and with each passing second, she continued to marvel at its power.

As they sampled desserts, she tried to keep her thoughts from running amuck. He'd made it clear from the beginning that he would not hold a girl's hand or kiss her unless he wanted to date exclusively. And here he was, holding her hand.

It was tantamount to a proclamation of exclusivity, and in an odd way, even stronger than a kiss. He continued to hold her hand, making no move to pull away. She wanted to ask him what it meant, to ask for a verbal confirmation, but wasn't certain she had the courage. It didn't help that the fluttering in her stomach refused to abate.

"I never thought holding hands could be so powerful," he said.

"Right?" she breathed, grateful he'd broached the subject.

"Do you want to take the blindfold off?"

"Do you mind?"

"There are a few more desserts, but I think I'd like to see your eyes."

She smiled and reached up with her free hand to remove the blindfold. She expected it to be dark, but she was assaulted with a vista of light. She blinked and shielded her gaze, and then she realized the source of light . . .

Thousands of paper lanterns filled the park. Fire twinkled beneath each, filling them with light and heat, making them expand and rise. Kate was surrounded by families holding several at once, the entire park blanketed with lanterns yearning to be free.

The slope of the park and their position allowed her to see the lanterns stretched to the base of the park, which had swollen since it had grown dark. She'd heard a shuffling when her blindfold was on, but her attention had been elsewhere.

"You held my hand to distract me," she accused.

"Guilty," he said, pulling her to her feet.

She turned a slow circle, her gaze sweeping the vista of lanterns. "What is all this?" she breathed.

"A Festival of Lanterns," he replied, his eyes on her.

Many were still lighting the fires beneath the lanterns and more glowed to life, brightening the already stunning scene. Light glowed and people laughed, the anticipation building to a fever pitch. She finally looked to Reed to find him holding the present she'd spotted.

"Open it," he said.

200

"Please tell me it's a lantern."

He smiled. "Open it and find out."

She reluctantly pulled her hand free of his and unwrapped the package, and found two prepared lanterns with a lighter between them. She eagerly ripped off the wrapping and they unfolded the large lanterns. Then he helped her light hers and she held it, watching the fire glow to life, the heat gradually filling the lantern. His lit as well, the fire reflecting off his face and twinkling in his eyes.

"It's almost time," he said. "Are you ready?"

Her lantern began to lift, yearning to rise into the night sky. She managed to hold it with one hand and reached out to him. He smiled and dropped the lighter in the basket, and then took her hand. Again, lightning arced up her arm and plunged into her heart.

"When do we release?" she asked.

"At nine," he said. "It should be about now."

A great hum filled the crowd as last-minute arrivals rushed to prepare their lanterns, some even doing so on the road between cars, unable to find a parking spot. Kids, adults, and grandparents, couples and families and individuals, all held their lanterns and waited.

Kate's skin tingled and she looked to Reed. His gaze was on her, his smile soft and open. Their hands intertwined further as the hum mounted, the people lifting their lanterns above their heads as they waited . . .

A shout rang out and someone released, the single lantern becoming a catalyst as thousands of people released theirs. Graceful and luminescent, the lanterns lifted, bumping and floating toward the heavens.

The people cheered and shouted, exulting in the breathtaking display. Children leapt about, the excitement bleeding into motion. Couples embraced, and more than one had tears in their eyes.

Some of the lanterns drifted lazily, others raced toward the stars. All were touched by the wind, which caressed and pulled, tugging at the lanterns and causing them to swirl. They drifted about, soaring in complicated patterns until the entire sky seemed a carpet of light.

"It's beautiful," she breathed.

"You're beautiful," he said.

She tore her eyes off the lanterns and met his gaze. He stared at her, the lights of the lanterns brightening his frame until he seemed to glow. She'd thought him attractive before, but beneath the tapestry of lanterns and light, he was like a vision from a dream.

He stepped forward and wrapped his arm around her back. Her eyelids fluttered as he pulled her in, against his body. She'd thought their holding hands to be the pinnacle, but she'd been wrong.

Energy coursed up her frame until she trembled. Every point of contact was on fire, the heat burning into her heart, her chest an inferno. His eyes were filled with the same longing. He leaned in, his warm breath brushing across her cheeks. She reached up and wrapped her arms around his neck, the motion strange and foreign, yet comfortable and perfect. His grip tightened around her back.

"What about your five thousand dates?" she breathed.

"I want them to be with you," he said, and pulled her into a kiss.

Chapter 5

All thought of the view evaporated as his lips brushed hers, a tentative invitation that quickly mounted as they closed the gap. Breathing became secondary, thought was redundant, there was only the kiss.

All the desperation, yearning, agony, and excitement exploded, each new contour of his lips leading to another tidal wave that engulfed her anew, the intoxicating contact scattering her thoughts into oblivion.

His hands moved across her back, pulling her tighter, pressing them together. His eagerness heightened her crushing desire, and she clung to the back of his neck, pressing harder against his lips. He pressed back.

She didn't feel the ground under her feet or hear the shouts of delight by those watching the lanterns. The wind was warm but heat came from within, and Reed's every touch caused her body to tremble.

After what seemed an eternity they parted. She opened her eyes to meet his gaze, his blue eyes piercing into her soul. Her smile felt like it would break her cheeks, and he laughed in delight.

"Worth the wait," she said, struggling to breathe.

He kept his arms around her back. "Are kisses always like that?"

"Hardly," she said, and then raised an eyebrow. "Am I the first girl you've kissed?"

"Third," he said. "But none were like this."

She laughed and looked to the lanterns, surprised to find them still hovering and swirling above. Their kiss had seemed hours long, but evidently it had just been seconds. Unwilling to release him, she used her chin to point to the sky.

"The scenery certainly adds to the moment."

"Is that all it is?" he asked, flashing a lopsided grin. "The environment leading to the kiss?"

"I think more experimentation is required."

He laughed and accepted the invitation, leaning in to kiss her again. To her immense satisfaction, the second kiss was no less powerful, albeit softer. She took the time to explore his lips with hers, and his shoulders with her hands. When they parted again she grinned.

"Is this what I have to look forward to from now on?" she asked.

"Does this mean you're my girlfriend?"

She smiled and pretended to consider the proposition. "I'll think about it."

He abruptly lifted and spun her about, eliciting a gasp and a burst of laughter. "You'll think about it?"

"Okay!" she cried. "I agree. I'm your girlfriend."

He set her down, a quizzical expression forming on his face. "You know, this is uncharted territory for me."

"That's right," she said, recalling that he'd only had two brief relationships. Then her smile turned positively wicked.

"What?" he asked warily.

"For the last six months you've been teaching me how to date," she said. "But you have no idea what it means to be a boyfriend."

"So?"

"So, *I* get to be the teacher," she said.

"Does the student get to kiss the teacher?"

"I'll allow it."

He laughed and kissed her again, and she found it difficult to breathe. When they parted he pulled away and looked to the mass of lights that were just beginning to drift away. The magic of the moment faded but their hands remained intertwined.

"Do you want to watch the lanterns?"

She wanted another kiss but reluctantly agreed, and twisted so his arms were around her waist. He shifted his hands so they stayed well below her breasts, a subtle motion, but a significant one. She realized that at no time during their kiss had he tried to touch anywhere but her back or waist.

She smiled, realizing that she hadn't been concerned about him doing so. With every guy she'd ever dated, she'd been on her guard, but with Reed, she knew *he* stood guard. It seemed new to have the guy be responsible for his hands, and she realized that was the way it should always be. When had she come to expect all guys to treat her with disrespect?

"What's that sound for?"

"Just thinking," she said. "Your hands didn't wander."

His expression turned quizzical. "Of course they didn't."

"Exactly."

He chuckled under his breath, but it sounded like he didn't quite understand. He tried to ask, but she shushed him, intent on watching the lanterns float to the horizon. With his arms around her, it was the perfect moment, the perfect end to the dating challenge.

The crowd quieted as all watched the lanterns rise into the sky, taking the light with them. Kate breathed a sigh of contentment, unwilling to leave even when people began to depart. Reed made no move to gather their things and they remained until only a handful of stragglers were in the park. Only then did she reluctantly sigh and turn to Reed.

"Even perfect moments have to end."

"Is that what this was?"

205

"As perfect as I've ever had," she said.

His smile was visible even in the gloom. Then he pulled out his phone and turned on the flashlight, using it to gather up the picnic. As they walked back to the car he kept a tight grip on her hand, only letting go when he had to get into the driver's seat. Then he reclaimed his place.

"Is it cheesy to say I like holding your hand?" he asked.

"I'm glad you do," she said.

He backed the car out and pulled onto the road, following the cars out of the park. Kate leaned against the door and continued to watch the lanterns. Like a collection of drifting stars, they sparkled in the distance.

When they left the park behind she turned to face him. "It's not really fair, you know."

"What's not fair?"

"Your dates are irresistible."

"Are you saying you didn't want to kiss me?"

She laughed at the absurd suggestion. "Of course I did. But you have to know what your dates do to a girl."

He cocked his head to the side. "I know, which is why I didn't let the dates become too much."

"What's that supposed to mean?"

He smiled and looked her way, his eyes sparkling with amusement. "That I hope we can continue to date."

She blinked in surprise. "You said our game was over."

"Do you want it to be?"

She considered the question, but the answer came easily. "No."

"Neither do I," he said. "We can go out on other nights and spend as much time together as we want. But every two weeks, we can continue the challenge."

"And outside that?"

He motioned to her. "You'll have to teach me. As you said, I have no idea how to be a good boyfriend."

"You know more than you think," she said, pointing to the pinpricks of light that were the lanterns.

"Nevertheless," he said, "I'll need your help to figure out the rest of it."

"I'm confident you'll be a good pupil," she said. "First lesson, kiss me whenever I want."

"That I can do," he said.

They left the mountains behind and he turned onto the onramp to the freeway. He accelerated and they left Denver behind, gradually moving into the mountains that would take them home.

"So, the rules have changed but the game continues?" Kate asked.

"Now that we're together, our options are limitless." He smiled, the expression tinged with anticipation. "The game is just beginning . . ."

Chapter 6

The man snored, causing the woman to look up from her book. She smiled and shook her head, but returned to her reading. The book was just getting interesting, and she settled in for the climax to the story.

A cooling cup of coffee sat on the table next to her, while next to her husband a second cup sat empty, its contents failing to keep him awake. Both were tired, but she had no desire to return to the comfort of their bed at home.

The machines around them whirred and clicked, occasionally beeping as they monitored the person lying in the bed, the sounds a symphony she'd heard so often they no longer registered. She turned the page, the scrape of the paper briefly breaking the stillness of the room.

An hour passed, and then two. A nurse entered and departed, her passage acknowledged by a smile and a nod before the woman returned to her book. The climax approached, and she was excited for the conclusion, her attention fixed on the story . . .

The blanket moved.

The motion was little more than a twitch, and went unnoticed by the occupants of the room. But the blanket had moved, and the fingers beneath moved again. Even if the woman had noticed she would have dismissed the act. "Random neurological impulses," the doctor had said on more than one occasion. But the hand stirred again, the blanket lifting.

The woman looked up an instant too late, failing to see the movement and only seeing stillness. She returned to her book, the excitement of the turning pages dominating her attention even as the woman in the bed grimaced.

Her eyelids fluttered, working to open as she rose from the deepest slumber. Her vision swam and the room coalesced into shape, her consciousness like mud, but gradually working its way to clarity.

The effort lasted for several minutes while the woman read and the man slept. Then the sleeper's mouth opened, her throat constricting, the vocal chords slow to function after three years of inactivity. She struggled to hold onto her thoughts and they gradually solidified, her consciousness continuing to awaken. She remembered a car flipping, then pain and the sound of her own labored breathing.

And Reed's voice, keeping her alive . . .

27 Dates: The Series

The Dating Challenge

The Dating Secret

The Dating Game

The Christmas Date

The Valentine's Date

Author Bio

Originally from Utah, Ben has grown up with a passion for learning. While still young, he practiced various sports, became an Eagle Scout, and taught himself to play the piano. As a teenager he began creative dating and continued the practice into college, where he took a break to do volunteer work in Brazil. After school, he launched his first series, The Chronicles of Lumineia, and has since published over 20 titles across multiple genres. He loves to snowboard, build treehouses, and play board games, especially with his family. His greatest support and inspiration comes from his wonderful wife and six beautiful children. Currently he resides in Missouri while working on his Masters in Professional Writing.

To contact the author, discover more about 27 Dates, or find out about the upcoming sequels, check out his website at 27Dates.com. You can also follow the author on twitter @27Dates or Facebook.

www.ingramcontent.com/pod-product-compliance
Lightning Source LLC
Chambersburg PA
CBHW030316180626
46810CB00003B/1111